THE CONGREGATION

D0873481

HASHIM CONNER

HcConner Publishing

CP

The Congregation

Literary Services by: HcConner Publishing

Cover Design by: Enigmagraphics

HcConner Publishing

In cooperation printing with Createspace.com

ISBN 1449986129

EAN-139781449986124

313.739.8107

hcconner@yahoo.com

Other Book(s) By This Author:

Karma

The Learning Curve

Author Information:

Website: www.hashimconner.net

http://conversations-with-hashimconner.blogspot.com

Email: hcconner@yahoo.com

Publicist: Sukari Harris

213.880.4171

Hashim Conner

The Congregation

ACKNOWLEDGEMENTS

I am truly blessed to have everything falling into place at the right time.

They say he may not come when you call him but GOD is always on time, and my career is a testament to that fact. I'm thankful to the women that raised me and brought forth the man that stands here today. The most important woman in my life whether we agree all the time or disagree she's the constant voice in the back of my mind that I have to ignore or listen to. Thank you Shirley Stephenson, better known as (Mom) I truly appreciate all the things you instilled in me to create an independent thinking strong black man. Thank you Lydia Alexander, better known as (Granny) for showing me that there was so much more than the hood, and that as long as I work hard for the things I want I can have anything in this world. Thank you Rosie Cook, better known as (Grannie) for showing me how important family is, because when there was no one else you stepped in and helped raise as if I was your own. That is something that I will never forget! You all are the sturdy foundation that all my values and goals are built on. Any success that I may ever have will be because of the life lessons you taught early on. I have a wonderfully huge family and to all of them I owe a great deal of thanks for their support. The number is plentiful much too large for me to name them all so with this remark you all will be included. Thank you to all of you who consider me family, I love you all. The thing about family is you gotta love them no matter what; you don't get to pick and choose who your family is. You just get to pick and choose who you deal with. With that said I have take into consideration the family that doesn't necessarily have the same bloodline.

These are my friends and nothing is more important than the circle you surround yourself with. The support system that allows you to be you. These are my friends that I consider family, and family that I consider friends. To my three headed monster, the three best friends anyone on this earth could ever wish for thank you. Nakia Magee, thank you for supporting me from day one! Letting me be me and not judging or constantly looking over my shoulder during life decision I have ever made. Whether I was wrong or right in the moment you rolled with me and then cursed me out when we were alone. You showed me what it meant to be a true friend and how I could be a true friend to others and that is something that I can never pretend to forget.

Michelle Jones, where do I even start with you it seems like we've known each other forever! Who would think it's barely been two years since we had our first real conversation. I can still remember the odd look you gave when I handed you a KARMA flyer and said "No it's not a Party flyer. It's for my new book!" You damn near fainted on sight, with a look of astonishment as if to say "Damn I didn't know you could read let alone write!" From that moment on we were damn near inseparable, and you've been with me through some of the toughest times and no secrets that no one but you me and the LORD will ever share. You have done what ya girl can only hope to do for Shawn Carter, and I thank you for the UPGRADE. Thank you for jumping on the band wagon and turning it into a Charter Bus because when you came aboard sales for KARMA rose tremendously. That still doesn't begin to tell you how much of a true friend you have been to me and I appreciate all that you have done and still attempt to do. I love you both!!!

This brings me to my brother from another mother Marlon Bradford (most of you know him as MB) first and foremost thanks for not suing (lol) If no one knows how hard it is to be my friend you do. There are absolutely no words to describe the things we have been through together. From working together to running the streets, you are hands down the Best Friend I have ever known. From the chicks, and the liquor to the uncanny wisdom that you exude in every situation. If there is anyone I would compare myself to it's you, and I'm in a constant battle to catch up or be better than my Best friend. Your silent demeanor says a mouth full. So with that said let's make sure that we have more fun every year then the fun we had the summer of 2005!!!

I have to thank Unck (Emmett Alexander), Tt (Amekia Alexander), and Tt Von (Yvonne Alexander) even though you all had no idea what I was doing with my life you still uplifted and kept pushing me towards success. I can't forget The Corner (Clifford Benton, Carlos Brown, T-Man, and Douglas Hill,) gotta love ya'll for life for supporting me when no one else did. The jokes kept me focused, even if you did have me editing the word

THE over and over again. The beautiful women of the Stepford Wives Club (Wanda, Wifey, and Lisa). To my siblings this is for you all, and it is only the beginning I promise once we make it we will never struggle again. I love ya'll and you all are the reason I do the things I do. (Jaquewda, Tanya, Danyelle, TJ, Logan, and Leah) like Logan said when I'm rich we all rich (lol). Love you all.

I also must thank my new friends in the literary world who have welcomed me and offered me treasured friendships. Thanks, Monica Jones, Dennis Reed, Stephanie L. Jones, and most importantly Sylvia Hubbard of HubBooks.biz. Thank you so much for allowing me to express myself and give your honest feedback. I hope my work does you all proud.

A quick thank you to my Atlanta family, and friends I am looking forward to opening this novel up to you guys first…Special thanks to Victoria Lowe (You helped so much!)

To my Publicist/Auntie, Sukari Harris, even when I am not on top of 'my' business you are. You have been involved with this project from the very start, offering advice even when I think I don't need it. Whether we agree with each other or bump heads, you still insisted. With your help I will make it to the promise land! Thank you so much, Beautiful for all of your support and expertise.   What   would   I   have   done   without   you?

Last but definitely not least I have to thank every HATER that I have ever encountered without you and your motivation NONE of this would be possible. So to every non believer, ever naysayer, and every person who didn't believe it could be done by me…THANK YOU!!! I know that sometimes I straddle the lines between Brilliance and Insanity but I have to thank the people who stick by me even when it doesn't seem like I am doing the same.

Thanks to the four F's in my life. My FAMILY, FRIENDS, FANS, AND MY FUTURE (Krystl White).

<u>Dedication</u>

This book is dedicated to the strongest young man I have ever met, against all odds he still manages to impress me time and time again. Life is rarely ever easy but some of us are so privileged and don't even realize it. Your strength alone compels me to keep my complaints to a minimum, I couldn't imagine dealing with the things you are forced to deal with on a day to day basis and the fact that you manage to do it without a complaint is enough to bring a tear to my eye as I write. If ever I am to idolize anyone it would be you Anthony Keith Stephenson Jr.

NEVER FORGET OUR DEAL!!!

Author's Notes

Some people say, usually with a puzzled look on their face, "You have a faulty stance or view when it comes to marriage." Well...I say...I have a realistic stance on today's version of marriage...It's definitely not what it once was the people involved have totally different moral standards and views. The world has evolved...why would we believe that with its evolution marriage would be the one institution to go unchanged.

Now...I am reaching out to write a novel.

Along my journey I have come to grips with some chinks in the armor of the marital institution. There are a number of things that are right with marriage. But just as importantly there are a number of things wrong as well. While on this journey I couldn't help but notice that people tend to get married for the wrong reason, and this fact alone is enough to ruin a marriage.

During my journey my imagination created these characters, as well as their problems. Throughout the writing of this novel there was always one thing that brought these characters together...One thing they all had in common...Church.

So...I named this book what I named the group...The Congregation

And that's what I would like you to be a part of...

Come on in a become a member of **The Congregation**

The Congregation

Introduction

The new in newlywed had definitely worn off in the relationship between Mark and Amber Coleman after only six months of marriage. Mainly because it had only been a few years after high school that they were rushed into a marriage purely because of circumstance. Though Amber's reasoning was true, the love she felt wasn't reciprocated, she was deeply and passionately in love with Mark. They were high school sweethearts though the sudden responsibility of a baby quickly changed his heart and both their plans. She knew Mark didn't feel the same, but hoped one day he would and they would live happily ever after. Mark on the other hand was getting married mostly for the wrong reasons he truly loved her, but he wasn't in love. His biggest reason for this marriage was the pressure he received from his father to do "The Right Thing" because of her pregnancy. As if being the son of a pastor wasn't enough now he had to take on the responsibility of being a father, a husband and a full time plant worker. College was out of the question now!

Terrance and Asia Williamson a couple in their early thirties, who quickly married after each, graduated from their respective successful college careers. Each of them having extended collegiate experiences because of the fields they chose. Terrance is a doctor at a local hospital, and Asia, was one of the Chief Financial Officers of one of the more prominent banks in the Midwest. Their relationship started off blissful, but soon took a turn for the worst as their sexual relationship or lack there of took a toll on the relationship.

Isaac and Veronica Patton also a thirty something couple. Isaac owns an insurance company and was generally a pretty stand up kind of guy; he was one of those "Say what I mean and mean what I say" types. He did well for himself after a more than humble beginning; his only mistake was falling for Veronica, the absolute wrong woman. To the average on looker she was the perfect wife, she was an active member of the P.T.A, a regular church member who was in the choir, and in her spare time she was even den mother to the local Girl Scout troop. Although with all this good there was also a bad side. A side that Isaac never knew about because if he did this marriage never would've gone forward. The one thing that each of these families have in common is the Third Baptist Church, to which all were members.

THE COLEMAN'S: *The Accident*

Mark and Amber both grew up in 3rd Street Baptist Mark as the son of Pastor Coleman who had been the pastor of 3rd Street Baptist years before Mark was thought of. Amber the daughter of Deacon Banks one of Pastor Coleman's oldest and dearest friends not to mention his right hand when it came to church business. It seemed that from the time Mark and Amber took their first steps, they were joined by the hip, because of the amount of time their fathers spent in the church. They went from walking and talking to playing tag as they got older and that escalated into a high school relationship that went a lot further than anyone expected. Amber was younger than Mark, by one year and after High School his loved waned. Mark moved on past their high school sweetheart stage and met some new friends, the love that he had for Amber was still there, but that was all it was he wasn't IN LOVE with her and there was a tremendous difference. Amber on the other hand would never feel this way about anyone else. She never considered they'd ever break up or he'd move on and so she waited. The news that she received after the accident was music to her ears. She knew it would be hard but their love could conquer all, and make a way.

As Mark limped into the room that Amber lay in with a look of astonishment on her face he couldn't help but feel like somehow, her being there was his fault. He felt bad but, it was the drunk driver ramming into the back of Mark's car, while they sat at a red light, which in turn sent them into the middle of the intersection and directly into oncoming traffic. With the car totaled they were lucky to be alive. Little did Mark know surviving the accident was now the least of his worries. Once Mark entered the room that Amber had been moved to and sat down she broke the news to him that would send his mind reeling. This was something he was not ready for after all he had a future to think about and every thought that he had never included Amber as anything more than a friend. Mark realized that his plans for his life had changed, forever. Pastor Coleman was from a different era and in that time there was no such thing as a "Baby Daddy". What would he look like performing sermons about pre-marital sex, and children born out of wedlock, and his only son is a prime suspect. He would fix this, and fix it the only way he knew how, he would marry them as soon as possible no matter what they wanted. With no objections from Deacon Banks, or Amber it didn't matter what Mark thought, he would always do what his father wanted him to.

After another long day at the plant, there's nothing more soothing than a cold beer and a stiff drink, at least that's the daily routine for Mark since he and Amber had now been married for a year. Now after his long days at work, he usually heads home to see the love of his life, and of course his wife is usually there as well.

"Baby girl, Daddy's home. How's Daddy's Baby girl today, is my little angel okay? Hmm, Hmm a goo guu gaga goo guu gaga."

"Mark I know you didn't just come in off the street and not wash your hands before you picked her up. She's still a new born and her immune system isn't strong yet. Put her down and go clean up."

"Listen Amber, don't tell me what to do, my mother has been gone a long time, and as far as my little angel goes I can pick her up anytime I want."

This was also part of the daily routine, walking into the house and into continuous arguments, mostly about nothing. Instead of Amber questioning him about the real problem, she would instead nitpick at every little thing he would do. This in turn would make him take longer to get home each day, and made his tolerance for her even shorter. As he made his way to the back of the house Amber stood partially in his path, pushed her hips out to barely touch his body. The mere touch of him was enough for her even when she wasn't happy with him. His touch alone was enough to bring a smile to her face. Mark knew this all to well, but if he wasn't happy there was no way she would be. The slightest touch sent him over the edge,

"What did I tell you about touching me all the time, I get tired of you always tryna touch me."

"Mark what are you talking about you bumped me. I'm not trying to touch you! Even if I did I'm your wife, and I should be able to touch you whenever I want to."

"Just because I married you don't give you an all day free pass to my body, so don't invade my space attempting to get free feels."

"What! You know what you don't have to worry about me touching you. I'll keep my hands to myself from now on."

"Good!" he exclaimed, grabbing a beer from the fridge and slamming it shut.

According to Mark and a select few women, a touch from him would excite anybody. He had an athletic build, although he could've been considered on the short side he more than made up for it with his build. In a lot of cases he was more worried about his body than anything else in life. His workout regimen would put many professional athletes to shame, and he knew it. The only thing on him that rivaled his muscles was his ego. Mark entered the bedroom just in time to muffle the sound of his cell phone going off, it wasn't as if it mattered or not, Amber would've never questioned him about the call anyway. On the other end of the phone was the thing that kept Mark returning home late daily. A blast from his past, so to speak. The young lady on the other end of the phone had been a past sexual encounter. That was until he found her on one of his internet excursions which was now a part of his daily routines. Nothing happen as of yet besides your daily conversations, and meeting on the internet every night after work. Though it was definitely getting closer to another sexual encounter each time they talked. The conversation was short and to the point, she just wanted to let him know that she had made it home safely and looked forward to meeting him online. With him expressing how nice it was to hear her voice, as he agreed to their meeting later in their special place then hung up the phone. Just as he dropped the phone on the bed, Amber entered the room apologizing for what happened earlier, and then asked what he was doing. Telling him that she could've swore she heard him talking to someone. Immediately explaining to her that she must have been hearing things, he once again cut their conversation short explaining that he was tired and wasn't really hungry tonight. So he would be taking a shower and then lying down. Without another word Amber agreed and left the room returning to the baby who, as if on cue began to cry.

WORKAHOLICS: *After Work Session*

Conflicting work schedules, and actually having nothing in common with the exceptions of church and the love of money has begun to take a toll on Terrance and Asia. Money, cars, and a beautiful home were all in their possession, but whoever said being well off is enough for happiness, was dead wrong. If there was any such thing as a truly miserable couple, they were it. Terrance seemed to always be at work, on call or on the golf course while Asia's job didn't afford her much free time either. As busy as Terrance appeared to be, Asia was that and much more. Her position at the bank had her leaving for work early and arriving home late not to mention the loads of work she brought home with her. Luckily, she wasn't married to a man who wanted dinner on the table when he arrived, probably because he was rarely there. From the outside looking in, there was absolutely no way to guess that these two weren't the happiest two people on the planet, but the truth was they weren't. There wasn't a lot of arguing, in fact there wasn't much conversation at all. Their communication was just about limited to public conversation. Anytime friends, family, or co-workers were around then their happily married charade would begin. No one could tell the difference, mostly because they had become so comfortable with the game that it had surpassed second nature.

Terrance finally made it home at a decent hour without the benefit of a church meeting, or a round of golf. To his surprise he wouldn't be there alone tonight, Asia had arrived earlier and was already relaxing in the Jacuzzi with a book she had recently picked up titled "Karma" surrounded by candlelight and soft music in the background. She was definitely allowing Calgon to take her away. Attempting not to interrupt his wife, he stood by the door admiring her beauty. Considering that they weren't the biggest talking couple in the world, there had to be something that kept them together. Terrance was no fool, he knew that one of the biggest reasons to stay was the fact that his wife very well may have been one of sexiest women he had ever laid eyes on. This fit into Terrance's life style to a tee. He had the best of everything, his house, his car, and his clothing, he even had the best in a woman. Not only was she beautiful, but she was intelligent as well, she was a perfect 10. While Terrance wanted and had the best of everything, he made sure that he was the best he could be as well. And according to the masses he did it very well, in fact his clean cut, sophisticated look is what had his wife and just about every other woman, he came in contact with, in awe. Not only was he a brilliant doctor, he had the physique of a model. Standing six feet four inches, and a chiseled two hundred and forty pounds he looked incredible. His skin a perfect match of brown that you could only find in a box of Crayola crayons, he was blessed with a set of teeth that would surely make any dentist proud. The only blemish to his otherwise spotless record would be one that only a few women would experience. He had absolutely no romantic IQ, if his mind, and body turned women on then just as quick his mouth would turn them back off. He had no idea what to say, or when to say it, and it got even worse when it became time to actually touch a woman. He would instantly become all thumbs. You would think that being a brilliant surgeon, his sense of touch would reflect that of a man with gentle hands but his does not. As far as sexuality went, Asia would definitely be considered the one in charge. She had the ability to make herself climax with, but mostly without his help. The two of them had absolutely nothing in common, except personal success it's a wonder they talked in the presence of others.

Between the warmth of the water and the heat from the pages of her book, Asia wanted nothing more than for her husband to enter the bathroom, and join her. But knowing the out come would leave her unfulfilled, she opted to fantasize about one of the steamy scenes in the book. Replaying each movement in her mind, she became aroused immediately giving her on looking husband a beautiful view of yet another one of her private sessions. Any other man in that situation would've definitely made a move to join in the escapade, but unfortunately for Terrance he wasn't one of those men. Keeping his distance, and allowing her to pleasure herself was what he did best and pleasure herself is exactly what she did. As her breasts rose out of the water then fell back under with each breath, Terrance could hear the slight moans of pleasure that he rarely heard when he joined in. Before long she was so into herself that her body began to move rapidly causing the high waters to sway, overflowing to the floor and bring her to the climax that her body was searching for. The entire time her husband stood in the door, without so much as a step forward. Noticing that her one woman show was at an end he quietly eased away from the doorway before he could be called upon for round two. Retreating to the bedroom, he was fast asleep before she dried herself and entered the bedroom. Asia thought for sure that her show was just a prelude to a long night of passionate love making, but in truth it was as close to a main course as she would receive unless she started a round two herself. Although she knew he couldn't satisfy her she'd always hoped that would change.

The Patton's: *Meet Veronica*

Isaac's mother told him years ago that she was all wrong for him, but it was too late, she had already dug her claws deep into him. Her image was etched into his brain, and besides his thriving business she was the only thing that he thought of on a regular basis. She was his world and no one could speak a negative word about her. From the outside looking in, there wasn't anything to tell, she did everything a good woman does. She was supportive, religious, caring, motherly, and on any given night she was as freaky as she wanted to be. He believed she was faithful, giving herself only to him when in actuality Veronica was living a double life that no one knew although few speculated about. With her husband over working himself, putting his insurance company in the forefront of the city's black owned businesses, she lived out her fantasies with just about any and everybody besides her husband. Starting with those close to the family and branching out to perfect strangers; she had a serious problem that, unfortunately she didn't have a problem with.

After pulling up into the garage, and quickly grabbing his briefcase Isaac noticed the warmth coming from the hood of his wife's car as he passed it on the way to the door. It was already close to midnight, and she should've been home more than enough time for her car to cool off he thought. He didn't jump to any conclusions just assumed that she had to run to the store for something. He had no reason to question his wife, he knew his wife's whereabouts ninety percent of the time, or at least that's what he thought. He entered the house making himself known with his usual greeting, "Where's the sexiest woman on earth?"

Wasting no time, Veronica appeared just in time to jump into her husbands arms throwing her legs around his waist. Kissing him all over his face and neck, her hair was still wet from the steaming hot shower she had recently retreated from. The whole time expressing how much she missed him, Isaac couldn't help but eat up every word. In his eyes there was absolutely nothing Veronica could do wrong. If he only knew that she had just arrived home from a rendezvous with one of her current lovers, he would take her off the pedestal that he had her so delicately placed.

"Aww honey, does my man want me to draw him a bath so he can relax from his long day at the office? Just say the word and it'll be ready in no time."

"There's no need for that baby, I think I'm in the mood for a quick hot shower, the quicker I'm in bed the better."

"I totally agree the quicker we're in bed the better!"

"What man in his right mind could argue with that? How about this I'll meet you in the bedroom after my shower and we'll see just how much you missed me today."

With only a hint of hesitation Veronica agreed to her husband's arrangement and retreated into the bedroom to prepare for a night of lovemaking. Veronica had a problem and it wasn't that she didn't love her husband, the problem was that she had a slightly greater love for sex. Unfortunately, she couldn't fathom having just one sexual partner, although she and Isaac had an incredible sex life, her body still yearned for more. The touch of a man was as unique as a finger print, each man has a different way of touching a woman, and Veronica was infatuated with the thought of these different touches. The different emotions she felt when each man touched her, the way each one made her body feel, was her addiction. Veronica waited for husband, she couldn't help but think of her sexual escapade from earlier in the day and with each thought, she grew more excited. As she recounted every touch, every kiss, every stroke from earlier, her nipples became erect, and her pleasure moistened. Gently brushing her left hand across one of her nipples, it stood up even further begging to be touched. At the same time her eyes closed and her right hand began it's descent to her lower lips. Slowly spreading them with her index and ring finger, she gently guided her middle finger to her clit inducing it to swell. As her fingers produced yet more arousal, her body began to move rhythmically almost forcefully as she brought herself to climax. All the while Isaac stood in the doorway of their bedroom with nothing more than his towel and a smile, as he enjoyed the beautiful picture before him. Not wanting to be completely left out, he stepped to the edge of the bed for a better view. Veronica hadn't realized he was there until he lifted her fingers into his mouth sucking them slowly, before pleasuring her wetness. As Veronica moved her hands from her moisture to the top of his head, giving him a guided tour, reintroducing him to the sights and sounds of downtown Veronica. With each tongue stroke, she fell deeper and deeper under the spell of her husband, until she couldn't take it anymore. She needed him, she wanted him, all of him deep inside her beautiful body, and he couldn't imagine being anywhere else on earth. Slowly raising his head from between her thighs with a devilish smile he began his ascent, stopping at her breast to enjoy her bountiful mountains. Allowing his entire tongue to slide from his mouth, barely brushing across her nipples; he allowed his full bottom lip to tease her nipple as well. The look of pure enjoyment across her face, she could no longer wait for her husband to take her to the place that she longed to be…..Ecstasy! As he finally arrived in perfect position to enjoy her lips, he kept his hips positioned perfectly to enjoy the part of his wife's body that had been used earlier in the day. Between the intense kissing and the anticipation of her husband inside her, Veronica was already seconds away from climaxing for a second time. When Isaac finally inserted himself her legs instantly began to shake and her walls began to tighten and cream. With each stroke she gently bit down on her bottom lip. While her other lovers never paid enough attention to her bodies expressions, Isaac was different, every expression she made turned him on and so he paid special attention to each one Veronica made. He had long been enjoying her eyes rolling back in ecstasy, biting her bottom lip and other tell-tale signs of pleasure that she made. The way she would throw her head from side to side and moan so intensely, was enough to push him overboard. As the seconds became minutes, and the minutes became hours the two of them enjoyed each other, until they finally collapsed from exhaustion. Rolling on to his side of the bed he admired his beautiful wife, Isaac couldn't help but express the love he felt for her. "I know honey, I know." Her arrogance was unbelievable, but accepted by her husband without another word. They each fell into a deep slumber.

Each couple had their own versions of happiness and each their own set of problems. The one thing that they all had in common was church. Where every Sunday they would meet and became part of a bigger family, the family of the 3rd Street Baptist Church and for a couple hours at least once a week the problems of their respective houses were not a big issue. Each week pastor Coleman would give a sermon that would speak to the souls of everyone in the building, he would convey each message in such a manner that even the children left with their spirits feeling full. Each week pastor Coleman's message somehow hit each person as if he was talking to them personally. He had a beautiful gift that could've come from only one place. Pastor Coleman wasn't one of those pastors who preached at you not filling you with the word, he was blessed with a gift. A gift that he shared with his entire Congregation week end and week out, a lot of the time whether they were ready for it or not.

Chapter 1*: First Sunday*

Being the son of Reverend Coleman was hard enough on any other Sunday, but it never seemed harder than the First Sunday. There were certain expectations for Mark on this day, not only had he graduated to heading the youth ministry, but he also taught Sunday school for the children under the age of ten of the church. Unlike the other couples, young Mr. and Mrs. Coleman were expected to arrive at the church bright and early to fulfill their duties and attend service. Just as he was every week, Mark was up bright and early rushing his wife. Though he never took part in assisting her, not even when it came to getting the baby and her diaper bag ready. With the exception of a "Can you please pick up the pace every five minutes.", finally after forty-five minutes of nagging from her spouse, Amber was finally prepared to leave. Any longer and she stood the chance of being left behind, or so he'd threaten. Although she was sure, he'd never leave her behind for fear of having to explain their absence to everyone, especially his father. Not knowing if it was out of the fear of disappointment, respect or a combination of the two, he always did as his father instructed. Finally making it to church and fulfilling his part of the day, by teaching the children the story of the three men thrown into the fire by the pharaoh, and through the power of prayer they were untouched by the flames.

The children ran to their parents and reported what they had learned in Sunday school. With Sunday school over Mark hurried down stairs to sit next to his wife and child to receive the word. No sooner than he sat down his father took the alter, clearing his throat and addressing the congregation.

"Good Morning church! He exclaimed

"Good Morning." Replied the church members half heartedly.

"I said Good Morning church! Now don't come in here playing, this is GOD'S time! Amen! Any other time y'all up and excited, don't mellow out now. If some of us was at the football or basketball game they couldn't pay us enough to sit down and shut up but now y'all sitting here too cool to praise. Some of y'all get excited by the thirteen hour sale at Macy's but once again when it's time to praise y'all holding that excitement in. Hmmm, not today! Not on the Lords day, he won't have it and neither will I! So I'm gone say it one more time. Good Morning Church!"

"Good morning Pastor Coleman", the church said in unison in a booming voice.

"Amen!!!" was the Pastor's reply.

Without hesitation Rev. Coleman jumped into his sermon, with every eye fixated on him, he had the attention of every man, woman, and child in the building, prepared to give one of his best sermons to date.

"I had a passage prepared for today, and I was so excited about it, before God whispered in my ear last night. He whispered and said,

"Coleman get up, get up and get your sword.

Before I actually heard him say it, he had already guided my hands to the page it belonged. Proverbs 18:22. Just as he requested that I do so, I am now requesting the same from you. Turn your bibles to Proverbs eighteen verse twenty two.

Follow me now!" he exclaimed, scaring a few members still looking for the correct page.

"Proverbs eighteen verse twenty two says "He who finds a wife finds a good thing and obtains favor from the Lord"

Hmmm, now I know the women of the church heard that one loud and clear. Amen!

(Amen)

Men we need to hear it too, can I get an Amen."

(Amen)

"Now this is where I'm tryna get it together, where exactly did we lose track of this beautiful passage? Where did we start treating our wives as if they didn't matter?

Let's dissect these words for a minute or two. Now the passage says "He who finds a WIFE!" Stop right there he who finds a wife. Am I reading that correctly? Does that say he who finds a girlfriend? Does that say he who finds a roommate? Yeah I said a roommate, because for you who are just living together that's all y'all are. If y'all committed to paying bills together, and laying up together then y'all should be committed to dedicating yourselves to marriage! But that's another sermon, altogether. Getting back to the task at hand, did the message say he who finds a baby momma? Once again no it didn't, it said, "He who finds a WIFE", listen to that for a second it's remarkable in itself. I'll say it one more time! "He who finds a WIFE" not he who sits back and dodges a good woman because he still thinks his stats aren't high enough. Y'all know what I'm talking about, so called men out here tryna have sex with everything moving while your woman sits at home waiting patiently, hoping you come to your senses. Or, you men who have been hurt by one of these women who have you so blinded by their beauty on the outside that the true ugliness of her inside doesn't show until it's too late. Now you wanna blame every other woman you come in contact with, for what that woman did. All of a sudden you don't trust no more, "hmp" if you stop being blinded by looks and actually get to know a person you would've seen that she wasn't what you were looking for anyway."

Pastor Coleman went on for over an hour, before bringing his sermon to an end. With the message ringing loud and clear to most. Mark sat their squirming in his chair as if the entire sermon was directed to him and him only. He attempted to look around as his father led the congregation into the prayer. Mark was hoping to find at least one person who was as shook up as he was by today's word. Unfortunately he had no such luck, though he knew he couldn't be the only person to feel the wrath of the word on this day. Although at that moment, he sure felt like it. No matter how much today's word spoke volumes of his life, Mark was at a point where there wasn't much that would change his mind. He felt like he had done more than enough! He was a provider and a good father. On top of that he married Amber and that was more than most men were doing these days. If that wasn't enough Mark was convinced that nothing would be.

Church was finally over for the day, but in reality only half of first Sunday was over. Dinner still had to be served for the congregation and at 3rd Street Baptist, if you didn't come for the word, then you were definitely there for the food! If someone was to put together a church cook-off 3rd Street Baptist had God himself on their side. He had blessed the church with three cooks, actually all the cooking was done by two women. The most important, or at least in her own eyes, was Mrs. Patricia Patton-Silver. She had been doing the church's meals for the past 14 years and had no intentions of stopping anytime soon. Her daughter-in-law, Veronica whom could do nothing right in her eyes, was just as good a cook as she was, if not better but she never complimented her on any dishes she prepared. The only reason Veronica ever stepped foot in the church's kitchen was to win over her mother-in-law. Unfortunately that was never going to happen, Mrs. Patton-Silver had Veronica pegged from day one as no good, and no amount of flambé, sauté, or crème boulè would be enough to change that mindset. Veronica may have had a chance if she wasn't married to Mrs. Patton-Silver's son but she was.

Dinner was as it always was, Fantastic! Every member that stayed over for the meal enjoyed a plate and some even went back for seconds. The beauty of 3rd Street Baptist was, no matter what was going on it was a church of the community first and foremost. It wasn't one of these new age churches that buy up land in suburban areas and then expect it's members to make it there the best way they can. 3rd Street Baptist was in the heart of the urban community. The doors of the church were always open and not just for service or to pass the plate. 3rd Street Baptist held its members accountable and expected them to do community work; everything from neighborhood study groups for the kids to feeding the homeless. If there was something to be done for the community you better believe 3rd Street Baptist had a hand in getting it done. This Sunday would be no different the doors of the church were open until well after eight o'clock tonight. So the church could fulfill there charitable work for the week by feeding as many people in the neighborhood as possible.

Chapter 2: *Mrs. Patton-Silver*

Patricia J. Patton-Silver! The way her name rings around the city you would think she was a political figure head. The way she sways through every special event that goes on in the city you would think she was born into money. Never in a million years would you guess that less than fifteen years ago she was living beyond her means, and was forced to live check to check income. But even then she was a woman with a plan, and her plan was raising the perfect son. Not like most young mothers where she was from. She wasn't going to allow her precious miracle to waste his life on a whim and prayer of some sport to get them to the top. Not her baby! He was going to be so much better, and prepared with a tool that no one could take away from him, an education. She was raising a strong intelligent black man, with more to offer than just some athletic ability.

Isaac was a mistake, well at least from Mrs. Patton-Silver's stand point. A better way to put it was he wasn't planned. His father by most rights would be considered a dead beat considering he walked out on Patricia before Isaac took his first breath. And he probably had a lot to do with why Patricia was so hell bent on Isaac not being some sports jock, considering his father was an all world football player that Patricia had met during her club hopping, searching for a baller younger days. She found exactly what she was looking for, a tall dark brother with a body as beautiful as a Picasso, and as hard as Mt. Rushmore. He also found what he was looking for. A one night stand and an early flight out of town. No numbers exchanged, Patricia was stuck with a real surprise, 9 months later. Although he wasn't planned from the moment the shock wore off she set-out to be the perfect mother and raise a perfect son.

Truth was that mistake, was truly a miracle considering her mistake forced her to take a new outlook on life. The pregnancy gave her new focus, and an undoubted test that she planned to pass with flying colors. Isaac was born and with Patricia's first look into his beautiful eyes she knew that her son was going to be special. The years flew by and with each passing year Isaac became more and more the young man she hoped he would be. At the tender age of fourteen Isaac was already acquiring college credits in math and science, and was excelling at all he attempted to do. Even the best school in Detroit didn't provide a challenge for the young man. Patricia knew this all too well and knew that it was time to move her son on to the next challenge. Which was also right on time because she had met and been dating Mr. Silver for the last six months and was growing quite fond of him and he was equally as fond of her.

The couple was soon married and Mrs. Patton-Silver could begin giving her son the education and life advantages he deserved. Upon marrying Mr. Silver, Patricia and Isaac's life changed for the better immediately. Mr. Silver was exactly what Patricia wanted, and there was no acting on his part. Through some very lucrative investments early on in his life Mr. Silver was in a place where he never had to concern himself with money again and from then on, neither did Patricia or her son. Early in their relationship the couple spent so much time and energy learning each other that Mrs. Patton-Silver forgot about her primary objective and Isaac unfortunately did what most teenagers do. He screwed up, and screwed up big! A couple months later Isaac was whisked away from Detroit Public Schools, and into an unbelievable educational experience. Through Mr. Silver's vast connections, Isaac was able to receive the best education money could buy, finally being exposed to a curriculum that would challenge him. That's when Isaac's studies forced him to be away from the church for a while, and also forced his mother to miss a couple months as well. When she returned there was an addition to the Patton-Silver household. Mrs. Patton-Silver had another son. Honestly it didn't even seem like nine months had passed, before Pastor Coleman gave the news one Sunday.

Half the congregation was in shock, especially the women of the church who thought they were closest to Mrs. Patton-Silver. They had no idea that she was even thinking of having another child, but it soon boiled over and most just chalked it up as a part of her new marriage. From then on you rarely saw Mrs. Patton-Silver without her youngest son Jason Silver. There was a slight difference in the way she treated Jason, than how she had treated Isaac, but the only people to notice were the older members of the church. Nonetheless she still had high expectations for both her sons.

Chapter 3: *Ending a Long Day*

Once the church's dinner was finally over, everyone departed making their way to their respective homes. This was the one part of going to church that Isaac dreaded, the drive home was long and seemed never ending. Especially considering the fact that Veronica usually had steam coming from her ears. Being pissed after church had become a norm for Veronica, and venting to Isaac about his mother and her treatment of her, was the norm for Veronica. Isaac tried to steer clear of the discussion as much as possible, which infuriated Veronica that much more. She couldn't understand how he never had anything to say about how his mother treated her. Standing up to his mother was never one of Isaac's strong suits, knowing that she only thought she was looking out for his best interest her intentions were good.

"Isaac I don't know how much more I can take from that........."

"Watch yourself, that is my mother!"

"Yes it is! And I am your wife! I see you're quick to come to her defense! But when it comes to me you don't have a damn thing to say!"

"What do you want me to say V? I'm never there when any of these conversations happen! What you want me to come in and just go right to scolding my mother? You want her to think you come complaining to me and I jump to the rescue? If you think that will make her respect you then, I will do that!"

"Well it would be better than you just sitting by and letting her talk to me how ever she deems fit."

"Veronica, do you want my mother's respect?"

The Congregation

"I could care less if she respects me or not! But she is going to stop talking to me like I'm some slut off the streets. That's gonna happen one way or another, either you are gonna stop her or I will."

"Veronica I'm sure you can handle it!"

"Yeah, I sure can but the question is will you approve of the way I handle it. Because she won't like it! I can promise you that!"

"If you think that's best Veronica! Just keep in mind you are my wife and she is my mother, and I don't see either of those facts changing."

With those last words uttered they both became silent; neither having anything else to say. Though Veronica was still burning mad, she knew what to expect from her husband. This was an ongoing situation that wasn't going to stop! Unless she stopped it, and this was the very last time Mrs. Patton-Silver would get away with disrespecting Veronica and she planned to do what ever it took to make sure of it.

Not having to drive far, Mark and Amber arrived home shortly after leaving the church. With Mark wasting no time acting as if he was the sleepiest man on the face of the planet. Not so much as a light conversation all the way home and it had no signs of picking up as they exited the car. Mark hopped out and closed his door without even a thought of helping Amber with the baby bags or even the baby for that matter. As Amber struggled to get everything out of the car she stopped for just a second. As if she was surprised by Mark's decision to get the front door open and walk in without so much as a look back. With the baby bag thrown over her shoulder and the car seat in both hands, she stood up and closed the car door with her hips, then climbed the few steps to the door. Walking in attempting to close the door behind her, she placed the baby on the couch and turned to go back and close the door, Mark was already there cussing and fussing.

"Damn Central air ain't free! Close the damn door behind you!"

Amber had no words; she just stared in disbelief.

"Could he really be serious?" she thought to herself.

What made things worse was the fact that she had made the payment after borrowing the money from her mother. She wanted so bad to go right back at him, but thought to herself what's the point. Her concern was for her baby, she didn't give her asshole of a husband another thought. Mark slammed the door shut, and then stormed to the basement. For a person who swore up and down he was so tired he still had the energy to check his email. Then Mark spent the next hour online while Amber attempted to put the baby to sleep. After the baby finally fell asleep, Amber laid in the bed waiting for her husband to finally come to bed. Unfortunately she would be fast asleep before he finally came to bed.

Terrance and Asia finally made it home, after having a wonderful day. Asia was in the mood to make the night just as good and for the first time in weeks Terrance was on the same page. As they both stood in their master bedroom undressing attempting to get more comfortable for the night, Asia couldn't help but admire her husband's beautiful body, instantly getting turned on by it. Terrance was just as excited by his wife's voluptuous body, her curves were beautiful and every one in their proper place. She was perfectly toned, and had the body to rival a woman ten years younger. Slowly and seductively undressing, Terrance enjoyed each and every movement. Asia gave a stare that screamed I want you and was even more excited when Terrance actually caught on. Asia had high hopes for the night and hoped that her husband could fulfill her passion. Terrance walked over to his wife pulling her close and kissing her deeply. This was the one talent that Terrance had and the only thing that he did that instantly made Asia melt. This time was no different, as she felt the pressure from his lips, her body seemed to overheat. She could feel herself moisten, as she kissed him back with just as much force. As their excitement mounted Asia felt the bulge of her husband on her thigh. Convincing herself that she was in for a night of pure satisfaction, Asia led her husband to the bed without breaking their intense lip lock. Terrance pushed his wife down to the bed spreading her legs wide, and buried himself deep inside her moisture. The initial entry of him was pure pleasure for Asia, she took a deep breath as she allowed all of him to enter her depths. Inviting her husband to go deeper; she spread her legs wider allowing herself to feel every inch of him. Asia was convinced that her husband was going to fulfill her every desire tonight. There were two unrhythmic thrust and a long pause. Attempting to keep control of himself, Terrance decided to pause, but as soon as he thought he was ready he began again, he lost himself deep inside his wife, letting out a sound so animalistic that every hope and dream Asia had for the night was shattered. As she felt the warmth of her husband exploding inside her walls she tried desperately to hide her disappointment as her husband went limp both inside and on top of her. Exhausted from this thirty seconds of work, Asia wished that it wasn't really over, but knew her husband better than that and knew that as unfortunate as it was, this night had cum to an end, just as quickly as it had begun.

Chapter 4: *Work Related*

As resentful as Mark was about the situation he felt his father had helped put him in, he would never stand up to him. He would never be disrespectful to him nor had he ever gone against his wishes. Mark had a wild side but his deep rooted Christian background kept him from indulging completely in everything his heart desired. His duties at the church, also kept him from straying too far away from his family life. But that didn't wane him from his computer activities, and now he even paid closer attention to the young women he worked with.

Outside of work it was almost as if Mark had a totally different life, aside from being the meanest and least understanding husband. He was becoming more and more disgruntled with his situation and the more disrespectful he became to his wife. To Amber the suffering seemed endless, no matter how much she tried, nothing was ever enough for Mark. Mark had a mean streak, and only one target to unleash it upon unfortunately for Amber. Constantly the critical husband, he questioned everything from the way Amber cooked, to the clothes she wore, and how they fit, especially since she had yet to lose the weight she gained from her pregnancy. He even had the audacity to question whether she was a fit mother. Mark had turned into a complete asshole. The only relief Amber had was when they were around others, then and only then he acted as he should all the time. He was loving and had nothing but kind words for her and luckily for her an enormous amount of their time was spent at the church, if he was not at work. She dealt with the verbal abuse because they were distributed in short intervals. Amber's low self esteem made her believe that she deserved this treatment. She witnessed her mother take the same if not worse on so many occasions that she felt this was just the way the male and female relationships work. She was constantly told to allow a man to be a man. Fed the unbelievable craziness that all men cheated, and that's just a man being a man. She felt she had no choice but to look past that, and work with Mark, or face being alone for the rest of her life; something her mother made seem like was the end of the world.

It was a long hot day at the plant and no one was more irritated than Mark. One of the older workers on the line couldn't keep up, so Mark was stuck working twice as hard to make sure the line didn't slow. Doing the work of two people didn't get him twice the pay but he was stuck doing it. The whole while staring at the old man a couple of steps away from him taking his own sweet time, on an unauthorized break was something else that Mark was stuck dealing with while respecting his elders. This wasn't the first time and surely wouldn't be the last. The only plus to working twice as hard was he started to get twice the attention from Roslyn.

Roslyn was his immediate supervisor, whom he had been noticing for the past few months. She didn't pay too much attention to him though, well not at first. She was tired of all the guys coming on to her and being disrespectful. Most of the guys swore up and down that she slept her way into her current position, but the truth was, she was really exceptional at her job. She kept everything strictly professional and because of that she had been labeled a bitch by both men and the women at the plant. She had plans, and unlike most of the people that came into the plant these days she was going to take full advantage of every opportunity. Working for the company had it's advantages, and a free education was one of the great perks that the plant offered. Most didn't, they usually allowed the seeminglessly endless money supply make them instead of making the money.

Roslyn had beauty and brains to go along with it. She understood that with the influx of machinery and computers the more outdated the workers would become. Soon the overtime that seemed abundant was going to dry up, and eventually so would the jobs. She was determined not to be caught up in those layoffs. The 30 year old woman had a three year plan and it included making herself so marketable that she could go anywhere and do anything once her time was up. With nothing left to complete but her internship at the hospital.

The Congregation

She began to take a serious interest in Mark, once he was transferred to her department. She was impressed by his work ethic and that he rarely complained. Usually when the younger guys come in they act as if they don't need the job, and were constant complainers. Most of them just get the job because they have family members that help to get them in. They rarely take advantage of the perks, just there because it seems pretty lucrative for them.

Mark was breaking a serious sweat when Roslyn did her walk through. She couldn't help but notice his muscular biceps ripple and tighten as he moved parts to and from the assembly line, pausing for a second, pretending to be inspecting the crews work. In a trance from the view she fell into a day dream. Thinking to herself "How nice it would be to have those arms wrapped around her holding on tighter than a pair of vice grips" she thought. Slipping out of her trance just in time to keep anyone from noticing.

"Looks like you're fitting in well on this shift Mr. Coleman."

"Yes ma'am I enjoy working this shift it gives me the rest of my day to enjoy." Mark said without looking up from what he was doing.

"Good, good! We are glad to have another hard worker on the team."

"Happy to be here!" Mark said this time, with a quick side glance.

Cutting the conversation short, she turned and walked away. Knowing that holding too much of a conversation would undoubtedly cause others to pay attention and that wasn't an option. Unfortunately for her, she was too late, to stop one overly observant worker. Mr. Williams spent more time worrying about rumors than any woman on the planet. He certainly spent more time thinking about rumors than he did work.

"So I see you got the attention of the H.B.I.C!"

"Huh? What are you talking about Mr. Williams? The H.B.I.C? " Mark questioned, obviously annoyed.

"You know what I'm talkin about Youngster! The Head Bitch in Charge! I see she giving you that special attention."

"No not at all she just spoke, and asked me if I liked being on the shift."

"Yeah! Did you see her speak to anyone else the entire time she was out here?"

"Yeah! She told yo ass to wake up!" Mark said with a snicker.

"That's right play it off. But you won't be able to in a while, soon you'll accept what I already know."

"Whatever! She ain't think twice about me old man."

"We'll see!"

Mark ignored the old man and tried not to think about the possibility of his statement being true. He couldn't help but allow it to run through his mind a couple more times quickly shrugging the thought off and getting back to work. It was the end of his work day and he knew he still had a long day ahead of him. Mark would've really loved to get home and hit the hay but he knew that wasn't much of a possibility. He told Amber that he would keep the baby while she took her mother grocery shopping. He still couldn't understand why she couldn't take the baby with her. He still was contemplating telling her that she was going to have to take the baby with her.

Chapter 5: *Near Miss*

Asia wasn't sure if she could sit through another one of these meetings. She was tired of sitting there being looked upon as if she didn't know what she was talking about. Being one of the few women executives at the bank was definitely wearing on her. On a day to day basis she was stuck in a room with a bunch of men who swore just because they were born with two nuts and a second head that they were better suited to lead. Even though most of them spent so much time with their lips puckered up to kiss the ass of the bank president it was hard to tell they were born with that second head. Lucky for her, this particular meeting of the minds or the mindless as she so smugly referred to it was coming to a close. She grabbed her brief case and made her way to the door. Walking briskly, she attempted to make it to her car without running into another moron, with something to say. While all the so called men spent their time brown nosing Asia's tenure had produced a continuous upward climb in the banks stats. She and she alone had convinced three of the five biggest clients to allow the bank to handle their accounts and the other two signed because she was on the board. So without the ass kissing she had become the banks most valuable asset.

Finally making it to the car she immediately jumped in and sat there a few seconds waiting, waiting and then it happened. Asia let out a terrifying scream.

"Shhhhhhiiiiiittttttt!!!!"

Thinking to herself now that feels better! She threw her Jaguar in reverse and then in drive pulling out of the banks parking garage. A right turn and then a left and before she knew it she was on the freeway and hitting speeds close to 100 mph, it was well after 7:30 so traffic was light. That was a good thing because she wasn't in the mood to obey the speed limit. She needed some type of excitement in her life and she was pretty sure she wasn't going to get it from home. So she might as well get it on the way. It hadn't even been five minutes before she was hitting the connecting ramp to 94 West and two more minutes before she was on 96 NW, three minutes later she was on the Southfield freeway North. She had just shaved 9 minutes off a 20 minute trip. Pulling into her driveway and hitting the button she noticed that her husband's car was unfortunately still there. The sight of it alone was almost enough to send her into another scream fest.

Looking up into the sky she mouthed the words "You just can't give me a break huh?" Grabbing her briefcase from the backseat she got out of the car and started towards the door. As she unlocked the doors she noticed something that made her change her tune. Terrance's bag was out and his coat was by the door, that could only mean one of two things either he was on his way out or he was just getting home. She looked up once again and pleaded with the man upstairs.

"You can give me this one."

Strolling down the stairs with another bag in hand, Terrance looked and smiled at his wife.

"Hey lady how was your day?"

"It was pretty good Terrance are you just getting home?" Thinking to herself I hope he's not just getting here! He better be leaving I want to sleep alone tonight.

"No honey! Unfortunately I'm on my way out, my nights just beginning. So I will see you in the morning."

Wasting no time he kissed his wife on the cheek and grabbed the rest of his things and headed out the door. Both of them knew the other was much happier being on their way somewhere else. While they spent a great deal of time keeping up appearances for others they didn't spend half that time when they were alone. They were quite happy with two different lives and schedules; it made life that much easier. Terrance was on call most of the day and had recently picked up a night shift to ensure he would have time away from Asia. Considering most of his surgical work was done early morning, he usually didn't have much to do during the night hours, so most of his time was spent in his office, or making rounds, checking up on the surgery patients from the days before. Unlike most surgeons Terrance was a breath of fresh air. Terrance had a firm belief that his patients had the right to know the person who had been playing cut and paste on their bodies. Most patients didn't care either way but from time to time he would get a person who was very thankful for his consideration. They wanted an opportunity to speak with the person who had actual answers not someone who just gave them medical jargon.

Terrance also enjoyed the nurses at the hospital, mainly because of the attention they showed to him. The same attention that seemed to be lacking at home. Most of them made attempts at throwing themselves at him, to their dismay. Terrance may have enjoyed the attention but knew better than to deal with any of them. As much as he enjoyed their attention he had no interest in being part of the gossip columns that surrounded the hospital.

The hospital social scene wasn't that different than that of a high school or college. Just like any other campus you had certain people "clicked up", with the interns being the equivalent of freshmen at any university. To many doctors they were nothing more than fresh meat. Considering the unbelievably high demands of the medical field, serious relationships were hard to have and even harder to maintain and a great deal of the participants were already involved or even married, making most encounters merely a sexual release. Now and again you would end up with an emotional situation and that was merely because the abundance of the people's time spent was at work interacting with each other. These situations were rare but they did happen from time to time.

Terrance was sought after on many different levels, not only because of his looks but his status as well. He was the surgeon that all other surgeons looked up to and those that didn't still showed him the respect that he deserved. The women on staff treated him as if he could do no wrong. Every time he turned around he was getting another look of wanting from another beautiful woman. Even patients would stop and stare at him as he strolled the halls of the hospital. Though he had never stepped out on Asia, he was beginning to wonder why? He knew neither of them were happy. The time he spent at the hospital would often be spent reflecting on his marriage, wondering when he lost his wife's attention. But he never could quite put a finger on it. Whatever it was, it stretched so far back that he couldn't even remember when or why things had changed between them.

After hours of work it was time for Terrance to do his rounds. This was his daily routine before he prepared to leave for the day. Lucky for him because he was being introduced to the shifts nurse interns. He spotted the very attractive young lady toward the back of the group paying more attention to the patients, than the rest. She was different, she seemed to ignore him, as if he wasn't even there, when with all the rest he had their undivided attention

Terrance left the hospital without finding out the intern's name, but knew that he would have many more opportunities to properly introduce himself. He was on his way home to relax after putting in his shift at work. It was a pretty uneventful twelve hour shift that left him with an abundance of energy. He decided to take full advantage of that extra energy by stopping into his favorite breakfast spot. Connie's and Barbara's was in the opposite direction of the house but well worth the detour. Not only did they have the best breakfast in Detroit, but Terrance was treated like royalty there. When he entered, it was as if Norm was entering Cheers and everyone knew his name. Although the breakfast at Connie's and Barbra's was delicious the true reason for Terrance's stop on almost every morning was to give his wife enough time to leave for work. He could honestly not think of anything else that had the ability to ruin his morning more than an early morning run in with his lovely wife. So a great breakfast and a quick stop at the gym is what his daily routine consisted of and today was no different.

It was the start of another long and stressful day for Isaac. As he re-entered the bedroom from his daily workout he watched Veronica lay there still fast asleep from the night before. Isaac paused for just a second to admire her beauty; even in her sleep Veronica was beautiful. He watched as she kicked one leg from under the comforter attempting to cool down as she usually did throughout the night. She uncovered her leg from her foot to her extremely toned thigh. Isaac turned away and made his way to the master bath to take his shower and finish getting ready to start his day. Turning the shower on full blast before slipping under the water sparked his senses immediately, his muscles were over worked and needed the beads of steaming hot water. Isaac dropped his head under the water and allowed it to take over. Enjoying the massaging water he allowed his muscles to relax. He had a lunch date this afternoon that had him wound tight and no amount of water pressure could relieve the emotional tension he felt. As he gave himself a full lather, the thoughts of him meeting his mother for lunch menaced his mind. Finally done with his shower, he stepped out and took the time to pat his body dry. Wrapping the towel around his waist and walking out to the bedroom he noticed that even more of his beautiful wife was exposed. Walking around the bed to his closet he nearly let out a large yelp as he stubbed his toe on the edge of the bed. Just enough of his sounds were released to get a reaction from Veronica.

"What happened! Are you okay?"

"Yeah babe just hit my foot on the edge of the bed."

"I was wondering how long you were going to stand there just watching me."

"I'm sorry babe I thought you were asleep, and I was just admiring my beautiful wife."

"Well thank you, but why the admiration from so far away. You should come closer."

A smile crossed Isaac's face as the pain from his foot all but disappeared. His focus had been snatched away from the pain in his toe and placed on more important matters. Isaac had been stressing all morning about his upcoming day. The relief that the steaming shower had failed to give him, would definitely be satisfied by a simple taste of Veronica's nectar.

With her entire leg already exposed and ripe for the taking, Isaac started with her feet massaging and tenderly kissing each phalange, then running his tongue gently up the side of her foot to the heel. Stopping for just a second once he made it to the ankle insuring that he circled the ankle so that he ended up on the inside of her leg. As Veronica smiled from the slight tickle of his tongue and lips, Isaac continued his morning journey. Already having his map route planned, there was a straight shot from where he was to his destination. Slowly moving upward and onward, he allowed his full and moistened bottom lip to lightly drag across her calves as he continued. Enjoying the softness of her satin skin he took time to allow his tongue to enjoy the sweet taste of her inner thigh. It was no different than biting into the sweetest Georgia peach. Isaac was oh so near and Veronica was aroused beyond measure, though she was no stranger to pleasure of all her indiscretions none of them could hold a candle to the gift of her husband's mouth. By the time Isaac finally reached his destination Veronica's juices were overflowing running down the creases of her lips. Leaving a gooey trail to her cheeks. A trail that Isaac was more than happy to follow to it's beginning. He lapped her juices up, enjoying every bit of her until he reached her promise land. Running his tongue around her beautiful lips, he teased them one at a time licking then sucking them into his mouth. Making sure that they were licked clean of every bit of nectar. Following the trail upward just far enough to enjoy her most sensitive spot. With only second of pleasure Veronica climaxed pushing all she had left to release out onto Isaac's bearded chin. Just as his wife reached her peek and blessed him with cream filling, the tension from the stress filled day that worried him was gone, as if she magically removed it. Isaac lifted his glistening face, with a smile of satisfaction pushing himself up and off the bed. He leaned down hovering over his exhausted wife's face and thanked her for breakfast. She gathered herself enough to respond, "No thank you."

With a new outlook on how today was going to be and a renewed pep in his step Isaac finished getting dressed. He strongly contemplated leaving his wife's taste around his mouth and her scent around his nostrils throughout the day. Deciding, Veronica's aroma may not be one he'd want to share with any.

Chapter 6: *The Meeting*

Isaac made his way to the office and to his surprise, started a wonderful day. Two of the major companies that he had been pursuing, had confirmed they would be covered by his company. This was great news and would undoubtedly take his company to the next level. Isaac was on cloud nine and he was pretty sure that nothing could bring him back down. Unfortunately in his excitement, he forgot about his lunch date with his mother. He was quickly reminded as Mrs. Patton-Silver entered the front door. The jubilation that Isaac had written all over his face instantly turned to a dismal look of dismay. His mother was not only keeping the date but was early. The room was quiet, as if the air had been sucked out, upon her entry. He walked across the room and met her with a hand shake and a kiss on the cheek.

"Mother I thought we were meeting at the restaurant, in an hour?" he asked trying to hold his composure.

"We were dear but I realized that I had another engagement at 2:00 with Pastor Coleman. So I thought we could move our lunch up a bit. Don't tell me you're too busy for your mother!"

"Of Course not, mother! Let me grab my things and I will be right out!"

"Good I will be waiting in the car." She stated turning to leave.

Mrs. Patton-Silver had become accustom to the finer things in life and no longer drove anywhere anymore, she had to be driven. The only thing that didn't changed when she married was church. She never allowed her newfound status to affect her duties in the church. She was still active and even more so, since she had become wealthy, constantly giving time and money. It surprised most that she continued to cook in the kitchen even after becoming the wife of a millionaire. What others didn't know, was Mrs. Patton-Silver felt she didn't have much of a choice, she had done so much wrong that she couldn't do anything but give back to the people who deserve it.

The ride from Isaac's office on the west side of town all the way Downtown was extremely quiet, as neither mother nor son had a word to say.

"I called Jason's cell the other day and the number was changed, what's going on with that?"

"Your brother does not need a distraction while he is in school. He is there to get an education not socialize."

"My brother, humph! Are you trying to tell me I would be a distraction to my own...Brother? I don't understand that!"

"He has enough stress with his class load he does not need to be distracted by you or anyone else. He will be home soon for break, well that is if he doesn't go anywhere else for his break."

"Somewhere else? He's not even in high school and he has the option of going somewhere else for break!"

"Well he has shown that he can be trusted, he's much more responsible than you were, at that age. With that, he will be given privileges that you were not. I believe you have more important things to think about besides you brother!"

"Things like what Mother?"

"For one, "that woman" that you decided to marry. Isaac I can't understand how you can't see that she is going to be your biggest downfall. She is going to break this family apart and in the midst of doing so, she is going to break your heart."

"Here we go again! What is it that you have against Veronica? What has she ever done to you?"

"Besides breathing? She made the decision to pursue my son and she is going to destroy him. I cannot just stand by and watch that happen!"

"Well mother you have no choice where my marriage is concerned Veronica is my wife and nothing you can do will ever change that fact! Deal with it!"

"Well my son the one thing that we all have to deal with on God's green earth is the fact that things change. No matter how much we might not want them to"

The car stopped in front of the Renaissance Center and the driver walked to the back door opening the car door and reaching a hand out to help Mrs. Patton-Silver out of the car. Isaac attempted to follow, but was stopped by his mother nonchalantly explaining that she had decided to dine alone. She explained that the driver would happily take him back to his offices. Isaac fell back into the seat and slumped down showing signs of frustration. He wasn't bothered by not having lunch with his mother, as a matter of fact he was quiet relieved by that fact. No, what bothered him was that he had allowed her to get under his skin with the least amount of effort put forth on her part.

Lunch had just begun for Asia, and she still wasn't going to be able to leave the office. Buzzing her secretary on the intercom, she made the request of ordering in a late lunch. You could almost hear the frustration in Asia's voice, being a woman in a male dominated world was getting to her. She was beyond pissed and was forced to suck it up. An emergency meeting had just been dropped in her lap and she had no choice but to prepare. For Asia that wasn't even the problem, she was the best at her company and did her job well. What angered her was noticing that the men were all working together, running from office to office preparing for a meeting they knew about in advance. Asia had two things on her mind, one was the serenity prayer, and the other was just as important.

"If we're supposed to be a company, why is it we never work together for a common goal. Why do we break off into our own little groups and try to come up with separate ideas instead of all working together?" She thought.

She wanted an answer to her question, but knew that if she took the time to bring it up she would be viewed by her male counter parts as emotional. Some may even consider her weak for feeling this way, so once again she held her tongue, biting down hard to prove that she is not only equal but the most important assets that this company has to offer.

As she looked over the information for the meeting, she noticed that the enormous and immediate problem that the company was facing was one she had brought to the attention of the board members more than a month ago. Taking another moment to realize just how under appreciated her opinion was, she was more than ready. She had the estimated figures and strategies already laid out. Maybe lunch outside the office was in order, as she collected her coat and purse, then headed for the door. She handed the file to her secretary and requested that she scan and make twelve more copies for the meeting, then told her that she would be back in about and hour and a half, maybe even two. With a smile and a yes ma'am, the secretary reminded Asia that her lunch was on the way. Asia smiled, and paused then said, well in that case charge it to my card and enjoy. Then turned and walked towards the elevator. Asia needed a breath of fresh air, if she was going to sit through another meeting of the mindless, especially if it as going to be a meeting that could've been avoided by listening to her a month ago.

One of the perks of working in downtown Detroit was that she had an opportunity to enjoy the ever changing scenery. Unfortunately Detroit was on a supposed decline according to every news station, and media center that had an opportunity to report the cities situation. They would think otherwise if they actually ventured downtown to see for themselves. There was constant construction going on from the renovations to the Casinos along with other recent additions due to Detroit being picked to host the NFL Super bowl a few years back. There were a lot of new spots in downtown Detroit that failed to get the publicity that they deserved. A quick journey across Jefferson and Asia was at the Renaissance Center where she decided she would be having her lunch. Ever since GM moved their headquarters down here and did a bit of remodeling The Ren Cen has been one of her favorite spots. They had a beautiful restaurant, Andiamo's that had a beautiful view of the river at night, and delicious food. As she entered the restaurant she was greeted by the maitre'de, immediately recognizing her for her frequenting the establishment and for her being a good tipper He rushed her past a group who was awaiting a table. Asia appreciated his tact, and slid a crisp 20.00 out of her purse folded it, then slipped it to him as she took her seat. With a glorious view of the water Asia sat and relaxed trying hard not to think of the meeting and the chauvinists she worked with. Having her waiter bring her a bottle of Cabernet Sauvignon and pour her a glass. Not wanting to over indulge knowing she would be going back to work she asked if the group of three women had been seated yet. Once she found out they had, she requested that he share her wine with them. The group had been seated closer than Asia thought as she could hear their response to receiving the wine. They weren't expecting it to be from another woman but they were thankful none the less. Never taking her eyes off the window in front of her she continued to enjoy her glass. The waiter returned and explained that the ladies offered her a seat with them, to which she declined. She wasn't there to socialize, she was there for a quiet lunch and an opportunity to clear her thoughts for the meeting. A very light lunch and a beautiful view was all she needed to return to work refreshed and mentally prepared.

Stepping off the elevator with a glow as she walked back towards her office. Stopping by her secretary's desk, she collected the copies she requested.

"Mrs. Williamson it looks like your lunch did you some good. You look more relaxed."

"You are absolutely right, it did exactly that! How was your lunch?"

"It was delicious. I just finished, before you walked in."

"Great! I hope you had ample time to enjoy it and if not, how about after my meeting you can cut your day short, and go home."

"Thank you, Mrs. Williamson!"

Asia entered her office and looked over the copies; she was more than happy with the work and was more than ready for the meeting. She left her office early with intent on being one of the first individuals there. Considering the President of the bank actually took time out of his busy schedule to fly in for this meeting it was a great deal of pressure but Asia was prepared. Usually the meetings are held via satellite with the banks vice president, but today was different.

The meeting started without a hitch, the president addressed everyone and spoke his piece, then gave the floor to the five people he expected results from. Asia sat back and allowed the men to stumble over their presentations, basically restating the problems and not giving any type of concrete answers. You could see the frustration on the face of the bank's President until Asia took the floor walking around the board and dropping in front of them a copy of her analysis. Not only explaining how they got in the situation, but also giving three different options on getting themselves out of the predicament. Her presentation literally blew the previous presentation out of the water. She also gave her opinion on which option would be the best for the company. The meeting lasted another half hour but it was actually over the minute Asia finished her presentation, she had wowed everyone.

Even after the meeting the so called important people were still basking in the glory of Asia's work. Everyone took the time to congratulate her on a job well done as they exited the room. Even the President stopped for a short lived conversation. Explaining that it was a pleasure to finally meet the woman he'd been hearing great things about as he gave her a firm hand shake and a pat on the back. Reminding her that she had a bright future with this company. Asia did an absolutely wonderful job keeping her emotions hidden, but inside she was doing flips! She was excited! As she quickly thanked everyone, then she left the conference room.

Chapter 7: *Intentions*

More than two weeks had passed and the time in the plant had felt like an eternity. Mark was sitting down for his lunch break having a turkey sandwich which was left over from dinner the previous night. Sitting there alone, Mark realized it had been some time since he had a word from Roslyn; she hadn't said a word to him since she complimented him on his work ethic. He was almost convinced by Mr. Williams saying she was interested, but he told himself to follow his first mind. She couldn't be interested; she had to know he was married. As he sat there enjoying the half sandwich and soup he had just warmed up. His mind jumped to a thought of Roslyn unclothed and a smile instantly crossed his face. Sitting in a slight daze he was still smiling even as someone walked in and sat down next to his seat.

"How are you today Mr. Coleman?"

Without looking up "I'm pretty good how about you?"

The voice had a familiar ring to it, soft and subtle but there was something extra there that wasn't any other time he had heard it. He looked up to find Roslyn sitting next to him looking as beautiful as he had ever seen her. She wasn't in her usual two sizes too big uniform, which kept most of the men from seeing her shape in its entirety. She was in street clothes and, they did nothing but accentuate her beautiful body. No longer would he have to use his imagination. It was right there all for him to see. Excited by the fact she was sitting next to him, but even more excited by the idea of her getting up to walk away and having the privilege of viewing that body in all it's glory.

"So how are you today Ms. Oliver?"

"Well Mr. Coleman I am pretty good but I would be even better if we weren't being so formal. Between me and you I would rather be called Roslyn by you."

"Well don't I feel special. Now what have I done to be so special? You know what don't answer that. But since we are on a first name basis, you have to call me Mark from now on."

With a slight smirk she assured him she would like nothing more than to refer to him as Mark. Then she winked at him and licked her bottom lip, then with a very sexual undertone she leaned in close and whispered.

"I'll call you what ever you make me call you Mark!"

Returning to her seated position and smiling harder than before her lean. Rosyln stood up before anyone else entered the eating area and started for the door. With a slow and steady sashay she made her way to the door but insured that Mark had the opportunity to enjoy the entire view before she disappeared for the day. Mark enjoyed every lasting second of Roslyn's exit before going back to his meal. As Mark looked back down at the table he noticed a piece of paper near his sandwich that wasn't there before, with a number and a message written on it. The message was clear, simple and to the point.

"(313) 432-1616 call me Daddy!"

Mark slid the number from the table and put it in his pocket and just in time, because no sooner than he did in came a group of workers. The group of men went on and on talking about Ms. Oliver's outfit and how sexy she was. Followed closely by what all they would do to her as soon as they were given the chance. Telling each other how they were the right men for the job of tapping that just the right way. Mark sat there listening and thinking to himself the woman they are all up in arms a bout just slipped him her number. For him it didn't get much better, the only question left was when he was gonna call. Luckily for Mark and his marriage the weekend was here and the demands of the church would definitely supersede those of his lustful heart.

Pastor Coleman's birthday was coming up and the church had been a buzz about this year's festivities. Pastor Coleman said his peace year in and year out about not wanting to be made a spectacle of for a day that comes once a year. The church rarely actually listened, and this year was going to be even bigger than the last two combined. The women of the church formed a committee, to plan the event. A last ditch effort to thwart the plans of the women Pastor Coleman insisted that Mrs. Patton-Silver be the head of the Visiting Committee. He knew that if there was going to be any type of planning for his birthday Mrs. Patton-Silver would undoubtedly be heading up the efforts. So if he kept her occupied with some busy work then, there would be no one to plan the event and he could finally escape the embarrassment. The Visiting Committee was a group of members that would travel to other churches in the city on behalf of the church. The Detroit Pastor's got together and came up with the program to unify the churches and communities, with the hope of uniting the entire city at some point. Visiting from church to church was only a part of the program they also offered programs for the communities and the youth. Putting Mrs. Patton-Silver in charge of something of this magnitude would definitely keep her busy, add to it the fact that she loves being in charge and Pastor Coleman had come up with the perfect plan.

The only thing that he didn't plan for was the ambition of Veronica. She saw this as an opportunity to impress her mother-in-law and at the same time show that something could be done in the church without the help of Mrs. Patton-Silver. The announcement was made by Pastor Coleman during the weekly Friday night meeting, explaining the importance of having someone of Mrs. Patton-Silver's stature in the position. She had no choice but to accept the role, after all who else held her stature. After Pastor Coleman made his announcement he excused himself from the meeting, feeling a sense of accomplishment. If he only knew that his confidence was misplaced, and a bit premature. No sooner than Pastor Coleman was out of the room, Veronica stood from her seat and volunteered to take on the responsibility of planning the birthday event. Asking for the assistance of only two constituents from the congregation to which she would like to decide upon. Mark being a member of the group wasted no time volunteering the services of him and his wife. Veronica not wanting her slight problem to hinder her ability to succeed in this endeavor she decided to accept the aid of Mark's wife but limited it to just her at that point.

No sooner than Veronica's offer was accepted by the members, she began running down her plans in her head. First things first she needed to decide on at least one other female to help her with the event and she refused to let it be one of the older women. That would've been the equivalent of having her mother-in-law on board, and that wasn't what she had in mind. She wanted someone around her age but not as dominant. She definitely wanted ideas and someone who could convey their point but at the same time she wanted someone who would have the same core vision that she had. She decided to wait until Sunday to pick someone she wouldn't mind working with.

Pastor Coleman had done it again; this week was no different than any other. Once again he had delivered an unbelievable sermon that had everyone in the church taking a deep look into their own lives. Even the holy of the holy had to take a second and check themselves after the work that was done in the church on this day. And just like any other Sunday it wasn't over yet, dinner was ready and everyone was invited. This Sunday's, sermon must've had a little something extra because people who rarely stayed were making their way down to the basement. This was Veronica's moment, she decided who she wanted the last member of her planning trio to be, and lucky for her she was in the building.

Terrance and Asia decided to stay for dinner this week, even though it went against their usual pattern. They usually only made church an all day event on first Sunday, but neither of them had heard the details to Pastor Coleman's birthday celebration. Knowing that it was coming up soon they figured if there was any information to be had they would get it at dinner. After all the after church dinner was a better source of information than the Detroit Free Press. As a matter of fact it was a strong possibility that this is were the reporters got their information from. Taking a seat at one of the tables closest to the door, they made sure there was a clear path to the exit. They refused to be stuck here for the entire night, as was the usual custom for those who set closer to the middle of the room.

Seeing her only opportunity, especially considering the clock was ticking with only two weeks to prepare she needed to take advantage of every minute. She excused herself and asked Asia if she could speak to her for just a second preferably in private. As the ladies excused themselves to one of the basement offices, for all of five minutes the deed was done. Veronica had her third member and Asia had all the information she and Terrance could ever need. As she returned to her chair she explained that they could now make their way to the exit. With a look of surprise, and satisfaction appearing on his face all at the same time Terrance removed himself from his chair and followed his wife to the stairs. Once they made it to the car Asia took the time to explain that she had just been recruited to help plan Pastor Coleman's event this year.

The weekend was over, let Mark tell it he had another week in hell to look forward to. Not only was there mandatory overtime, but add to that his possible baby sitting duties and his week was screwed. Mark loved his daughter and she was the most important person on earth to him, but having to watch her for hours drove him crazy. Especially after a hard day at the plant coming home to a baby who can't tell you what they want is a hard thing to look forward to. Mark was still unable to think of what came over him when he volunteered Amber's services for the planning of the upcoming event. Just then a picture of Veronica flashed through his head and he remembered just were his thoughts were. Veronica was sexy as hell, and he would've loved to be working long nights along side of her. He was hoping she picked him and no one else that would've been perfect. The flash of Veronica lasted a minute too long before Mark was interrupted by his line mate.

"Wake up boy! Stop day dreaming we don't have time for that!"

Thinking to himself "Ain't that a bitch!" As many times as he has had to cover that old ass man, by working twice his normal pace to make sure the line didn't fall behind for this old ass slacker. He had the audacity to tell him they didn't have the time for something! Just that quick Mark's usually innocent facial expressions had an immediate overhaul. As he opened his mouth to respond he noticed out of the corner of his eye that Roslyn was walking into their work station. Forced to hold his tongue Mark just stared at the older gentleman, then got right back to work. Roslyn walked up and told Mark she would need to see him in her office. So distracted by the comments of Mr. Williamson Mark didn't think twice about what Roslyn might have wanted. Leaving the line and walking into her office his thoughts still weren't clear.

"Hello Mr. Coleman. How are you today?"

"I'm good ma'am."

"Ma'am? Mr. Coleman I know this is a professional environment but I am not even close to being old enough to be considered a Ma'am. Roslyn is fine."

"Okay, well I am fine Roslyn. How are you today?"

"Well that depends Mr. Coleman."

"On what Mma....? I mean Roslyn. Since we're on a first name basis call me Mark"

"You of course Mark...It all depends on you I was wondering why you haven't used what I gave you yet?"

Stunned by Roslyn's forwardness Mark was speechless, he had never had a woman be as forward as Roslyn was being in this instance. Searching his mind for a witty comeback, and thinking for a split second that he had one Mark opened his mouth.

"Well I'm married."

Wait, that wasn't what he meant to say. That wasn't the witty comeback that Mark just knew he was going to get back control of the conversation with. With a devilish smirk Roslyn looked directly in Mark's eyes and responded.

"So! That doesn't concern me, I am only interested in one side of your marriage. Actually I am only interested in one side of you. Mark are you enjoying working this shift?"

"Ummm, I......"

"Before you answer Mark let me rephrase the question. Would you like to continue to work on this shift?"

Once again Mark was at a lost for words. He stood there with a look of bewilderment etched across his face. He wanted to answer, but wanted to be sure that his words came out the right way this time. Mark was more than interested in Roslyn but didn't appreciate her taking this route with him. Finally getting his response together, he thought just a second more. But it was too late, Roslyn couldn't hold it in any longer she burst with laughter. Pointing and laughing at the same time she uttered the words.

"You should've seen your face! I am so sorry I just couldn't help myself I wanted to see what you were gonna say and do. But I couldn't hold it in any longer. I am so sorry! I hope you're not upset."

Mark didn't know how to respond, he was sick about it, but he had to admit she had him going. The two of them laughed for the next couple of minutes before Mark turned around to go back out to his job. Roslyn actually didn't want anything at all just to talk for a bit. Though she did stop him at the door and gave him the sign to give her a call, using her thumb and her pinky as if her hand was a telephone.

Mark wasted no time getting deep into work once he made it back to his station. He knew that if he didn't Mr. Williams would definitely have something to say. Mark was in no mood to listen to the ramblings of the old man. There was no denying anything anymore Mark couldn't play dumb as far as his boss went. She had made her interest apparent, even if she did it in the form of a joke. Of course the only two people that needed to know of their situation were them. So as far as Mr. Williams was concerned Mark still would pretend to be dumbfounded. Mark knew one thing, if he knew nothing else, he knew he'd be giving Roslyn a call later on tonight.

After making it through an impossibly long week and an even longer weekend. Isaac was relieved to be able to just relax with this week's schedule being a bit less hectic. Most importantly he didn't have to deal with his mother this week and that was a blessing in itself. Being appointed to the new position Pastor Coleman insisted she take was truly a blessing for all. At least now someone else would have to deal with her driving them crazy for a while. Isaac had plans of his own this week, since both his mother and wife would be busy with events they were planning. Isaac decided that there was no time like the present to see Jason. There was no way he would accept his mother's words on this, after all Jason was his brother. And there is not that much studying to do in the world. Isaac knew all too well what it was like to be isolated at an all boys school with no hint of escape, and now no means of communication to the outside world. Jason had to be going crazy!

If there was one person besides his mother who had contact with Jason it was Mr. Silver. He was also the only person who had some kind of control over Isaac's mother. Although limited Mr. Silver did have the ability to rein his wife in at least a bit more than anyone else. Isaac called his stepfather to get his brother's number, with a quick conversation and Mr. Silver's usual warning. Isaac was so used to the warning he pretty much mouthed the words with his stepfather.

"Be careful son it's wild out here."

Heeding the warning and saying their good-byes, Isaac had the number and was ready to talk to Jason. Jason was a bit different from Isaac; he was much more outgoing and even more athletic. The beautiful part about going away to an all boys schools was the fact that what your parents didn't know didn't hurt them. The strict rules of Mrs. Patton-Silver didn't quite reach Jason all the time; add that to Jason being more daring than his brother had ever been. There was no way Jason wasn't going to play sports in school, it didn't help that his talent level had more than surpassed his peers. Jason was so talented, that the school allowed him to get away with a couple of things that most students couldn't. The main one being no consent from "Mommy Dearest." Any information needed for him to participate in sports went directly to Mr. Silver who could never bring himself to tell his son "no." His phone rang twice before he picked up.

"Isaac, hey big bro! What's going on.?"

"Nothing much Lil' Bro! Just calling to check on you, mom said you were studying like crazy."

"Oh yeah? Is that what she said?" Well we both know the expectations of the great Mrs. Patton-Silver! You'd think she was grooming me to be the second black president or something."

"Oh you didn't hear that is the new plan for you. Once Barack got elected your future automatically changed."

The brothers both took the time to laugh about their mother's expectations, even though they both knew their words had so much truth in them. The conversation continued for about twenty minutes before

Jason interrupted and explained that he would have to go in a few minutes. Isaac decided to throw out his last question before they would be getting off the phone.

"So I hear you're not coming home for the holidays? What up with that? You going out of town?"

"Aaaa....well....I....um, yeah I am going to a friend's house for the holidays."

"Is that right? Sounds a little suspect. Jason you know I can tell when you're lying. Hell a deaf person can hear when you're lying."

"Well Bro' you gotta promise not to tell Mom!"

"Okay, no problem."

"No Mark, promise you won't tell you know Mom! She would pitch a fit if she found out and she would kill both of us. Me for doing it, and you for knowing about me doing it."

"What the hell are you doing Jason!"

"Nothing to worry about, I play football and I am going to play basketball in the winter. But you know how she feels about sports. She would've never agreed to let me play."

"You are absolutely right! So how are you doing it and she doesn't know?"

"That's the beauty of being three hours away. I got dad to sign everything and he promised not to say anything. But I have to go right now we have practice in about thirty minutes and I still have homework."

"So wait! Are you any good?"

"Well consider this I am not even in high school yet and I am ranked as one of the top25 players in the state and 15 of the people on the list are seniors. I am going on a trip with the team instead of coming home for the Holiday's"

"Wow! That's exciting when can I come up for a game?"

"I'll be sure to let you know! But I gotta go. Talk to you later Big Bro!"

"Okay, Lil bro! Talk to you later."

Isaac hung up the phone impressed not only by his younger brother's talent, but his willingness to do what he wanted regardless of what their mother thought. That was the one thing Jason did on a regular basis that Mark often wished he had the backbone to do as well. To be honest if it wasn't for Jason, Mark probably wouldn't have the courage to go against his mother and marry Veronica.

Today was the big day, it was the first meeting for the event and Veronica had the house spotless! She had been cleaning all day preparing for tonight's planning party. She had finger food and wine for her two guest and had been writing out plans for the past two hours. She wasn't expecting anyone until 7:00 considering it was a work night, but just in case she had an early bird she had everything ready at 6:00. Good thing she did, because she had an early bird. Veronica's phone rang with Asia on the other end confirming the address as she was about to enter it in her car's navigation system. She also wanted to give Veronica a heads up, that she would be a bit early if that was okay.

Asia had just got off work and knew that if she went home first she would be late or not make it at all. With no complaints Veronica recited the address, and asked Asia if she would like her to have a glass of wine ready. Expressing just how bad she could use a glass to take the edge off, Asia thanked Veronica in advance for her hospitality.

Asia didn't waste much time after their conversation, soon after there was a knock on the door. Veronica answered with a hug and a glass for her first guest as they retreated back into the dining room. Veronica had everything set up, with three stations set up on the table each with a pen and notebook. No sooner than they sat down and Asia finished her first glass there was another tap at the front door. Veronica excused herself expecting Amber to be at the door. Inviting Amber in with the same greeting that Asia had received Veronica showed Amber into the dining room. As the ladies sat and discussed the plans for the upcoming event they also got familiar with each other. Learning as much as possible about their new partners in planning.

Once Amber walked in and got comfortable each lady introduced themselves to each other. Giving a bit of background, then allowed Veronica to take over the meeting. Veronica took the time to explain why she decided to take on the challenge, and why she chose each of them. Being sure not to reveal the main reason for taking on the job, this was to out do her mother-in-law. She did however let them know that this extravaganza was to be by far the best ever planned. She made it clear she was planning to blow any previous event out of the water. Veronica started to go over a couple ideas without actually going deep into them, as the ladies sat and listened. It wasn't until Amber interjected, and asked for the restroom because the little bit of wine that she had sipped had ran through her. After telling her the directions to the restroom Veronica and Asia both glanced at each other then almost simultaneously snickered. Not believing that she could only have had three small sips at the most how quickly she was ready to use the bathroom. Each of them had been on their third glass and heading to their fourth. By the time Amber returned from the ladies room, she was in the midst of a totally different conversation. Veronica was now telling about all the different clubs and groups she was a part of.

Urging the woman to tell a little bit more about themselves, since they would be working together quite closely for the next two weeks. They started with Amber, both women insisted on knowing just what it was like to be married to the Pastor's son. The questions were light, and random until Veronica opened the floor completely by asking if it was 24/7 choir boy or was he actually a regular guy. Amber blushed for a second and to insure that she didn't ruin her husband's good name she agreed with the choir boy comment. That was until Asia threw her two cents into the discussion.

"He can't be too much of a choir boy, I see that beautiful little lady with y'all at church every week."

Both Veronica, and Asia smiled then laughed. Amber reached for her glass of wine cracking a smile realizing that the jokes were harmless, and innocent. The ladies were getting more and more comfortable with each other. They became more open without revealing too much about their personal lives. The ladies spent the next two and a half hours sitting and talking. They called themselves planning but because of the wine the conversations really didn't go that route. A great deal of their time was spent discussing each other. It started with Asia explaining how difficult life was working in a field dominated by men. How every decision she makes is second guessed by everyone, even though she has looked at every angle possible before she presents it. Not having a full grasp of what Asia was talking about the other two women just listened and agreed.

Mark wasted no time once he made it home, he went in for the kill while he still had some energy left. He had been tuckering his beautiful daughter out for the past hour an a half and it was finally working. They had played peek-a-boo until she had no more peek and he was all out of boo. She had also been fed, burped, and changed and was ready for at least a good two hours of nap time. Now all Mark needed was something to keep him entertained for the next hour or so until his wife returned home. He was on watch and while on watch with his precious daughter there could be no sleep time. Thinking to himself what better time than now to introduce himself by phone to Roslyn? He really didn't feel like talking on the phone so he decided to send a text.

"Hey boss!"

Mark sat back and flipped on the television, the beauty of texting was not only could you hold a complete conversation but you could also continue whatever you were doing at the time. So if you were watching your favorite show, you weren't disturbed. That was totally different from actually talking on the phone. On the phone you had to be paying attention, because if not you would be stuck with a bunch of "Huh? Or What did you say?, or the worst one I didn't hear you can you say that again?" But not with texting everything can be read two or three times and you still don't have to ask anyone to repeat themselves. Only catch is you lose a lot in texting, the inflection in people's speech that allows you to know how they meant certain statements! This was an immediate problem for Mark as Roslyn responded to his text.

"I'm not your boss!'

Stumped for a second, Mark couldn't decide how to respond to her statement. It wasn't until she texted again with an "Lol" that he realized it was just fun and games. Mark and Roslyn held a text conversation for the next hour back and forth, back and forth. Roslyn finally ended the conversation because she had studying to do before the night came to an end. Mark had the baby tuckered out and asleep, and was just about ready to lay down and do the same but he knew that wasn't an option. At least not until his wife returned home. Mark was waiting for his wife, when his phone lit up with another message. This time there was no text he had a picture message from Roslyn, who he thought for sure had studying to do. Mark opened the message to find a picture of the beautiful woman smiling with the caption underneath saying "This is what you made me do when you texted." Mark couldn't help, but crack a smile himself as he replied to the message.

"Well I am more than happy that I could help put a smile on your face. And I look forward to doing so much more!"

"Really? Well if that is the case why don't you show me something that will keep me smiling?"

"Well why don't you help me out? What would put a smile on that pretty face of yours?"

"Hmmm surprise me!"

Not really sure how far he should go with this game Mark thought for a couple minutes on it. He had taken this game pretty far with women on his chat lines showing pictures of parts of him that only his wife should have the privilege of seeing. He wasn't sure if Roslyn was expecting anything of that nature so he decided to keep his pictures PG-13. Coming to the conclusion that if she wanted to see more she should ask him for it! Taking a headshot of himself exposing nothing but his head and shoulders, then sending to his new text buddy Mark had a devilish smile on the photo. Typing in the caption below, is this good enough? As Roslyn awaited the picture to come through she sat pondering just how far Mark had gone in his attempt at making her smile. The picture came through and indeed was enough to make her smile but she was hoping for a bit more. Still she thanked him for putting a smile on her face and keeping her company while she was stuck working on the homework. Mark responded thanking her for the opportunity to keep her company then told her to get her work done.

The meeting was over and Amber was about ten minutes from the house when she called Mark to make sure he didn't need anything while she was out. It was already dark by now, which would've stopped most men from having their wife stop for anything. Mark however wasn't most men, he asked Amber to stop and grab him some chicken tenders. Amber didn't have a problem with the request, and made a quick pit stop for her husband. Amber ordered the chicken tenders but for the life of her couldn't remember what sauce Mark usually got. Just to make sure she didn't get the wrong thing she asked for two of both sauces. She got two honey mustard and two sweet and sour. Pulling away from the drive-thru thinking to herself I hope he doesn't want barbeque. She eased her mind, by remembering that there was some barbeque sauce in the refrigerator that was left over from a couple weeks ago. Amber pulled up in the drive-way expecting that her husband would be at the door to make sure she got in the house safely. Then she remembered who she was married to, as she got in the house and place Mark's bag on the kitchen table he entered the kitchen.

"Hey Amber. How was the meeting?"

"It wasn't bad Veronica and Asia are both really nice."

"So did you guys get the event together?"

"We aren't done yet, Veronica has big plans for the event she wants to make it really fancy. So we will probably be meeting a couple more times this week and next week."

"What? How long is this gonna take? I know you can't expect me to watch the baby every time?"

"Well Mark I thought it wouldn't be a problem. After all you volunteered me for this, and it is for your father."

"You still have responsibilities to this household! What you think just because the event is for my father it excuses you from being a mother?"

"What? What are you talking about Mark? I am a mother to my daughter."

"What ever Amber! You just remember who is the head of this household!"

Mark reached into the bag and pulling out the four sauces, then reading them Mark hit the roof!

"What is this? You know damn well I don't eat anything but barbeque sauce! Who the hell eats honey mustard or sweet n sour on chicken fingers? You can't even get a simple order right with yo worthless ass!"

Amber wanted so badly to say what was on her mind at that second but as usual she took the verbal abuse. Then walked over to refrigerator and pulled out a bottle of tangy barbeque sauce and slammed it on the table. Mark looked at the bottle and yelled "It ain't the same!" Just then he threw the chicken fingers back in the bag refusing to eat them. Mark stormed down the stairs for a night of internet chatting.

Chapter 8: *Fantasize*

Beautiful as the last day he saw her. At least she seemed to be Isaac still had trouble making out her face completely because of the thick mist. He tried to get closer but the closer he got the further away she seemed and the thicker the mist became. It couldn't be her, there was absolutely no way. But he knew that walk, and the bounce of her hair, however he just couldn't see her face. Frustrated Isaac picked up his pace, wanting and needing to get closer. He had to know if it was her, still thinking to himself as he briskly walked in her direction. He seemed as if he was finally making up some ground. Maybe she noticed him, maybe she knew it was him, was it really her. Finally he reached her and grabbing her shoulder, attempting to spin her around. And just as he placed his hand on her shoulder and started to say her name.

"Sha......."

She turned but before Isaac could make out the face he was hoping for he awoke. Immediately sitting up in his bed, he was at home lying there with his wife next to him. Taking a glance at the clock he noticed it read 4:45 am, and it had happen again. This was the same dream that had haunted him in his sleep for the past week. Once again waking him up at the same time, as Isaac slid from beneath the sheets he made sure not to wake his sleeping wife. As Isaac made his way to the bathroom to throw a bit of water on his face to fully wake himself from the sleep he had barely enjoyed. Still thinking what on earth the dream could've possibly meant, and why did he keep having it time and time again? With sleep being the last thing on his mind, Isaac decided that a little stress relief was in order. He headed down for his morning workout, it seemed to be the only thing that would calm him besides waking Veronica and having his way with her. Exiting the room being sure not to wake his wife, still baffled by the dream that had woke him again.

Thirty minutes running uphill on the tread mill, to get his heart pumping followed by a hard workout on the bench. Isaac usually worked out with about 135, it wasn't a lot but it was definitely enough for what he wanted to do. Instead of increasing the weight as he went along Isaac increased the reps. He was into tone not bulk. After working his arms and chest for about twenty minutes, Isaac was back on cardio for his cool down. Jumping on the stationary bike for a thirty minute ride. Hour and a half later Isaac is on his way to his shower soaked from his own sweat. Still running through his mind was the dream that woke him this morning, and even after his workout his mind was still in a state of unease.

As Isaac entered the room Veronica rolled over to greet her husband.

"Good morning baby."

"Hey Hun, I apologize if I woke you I was trying to keep it down."

"It wasn't you I rolled over and saw that you weren't there that's all. How was your workout this morning?"

"It was a good one. I'll be paying for it later on. I can already feel my arms tightening up on me now. So how did the meeting go last night?"

"I think it went well. We spent some time getting to know one another, since we are gonna be working together for the next couple weeks."

"I assumed it went pretty well because when I got home I noticed about six empty bottles of wine, and you were already fast asleep."

"Six? Are you serious? I thought we only went through three. Wow! Well it was worth it! I think I did a good job recruiting these ladies. We are going to get along great."

"Why because you all drink?"

"No, Mr. Comedian! As a matter of fact, Amber didn't even drink that much. Now Asia was a different story. She was throwing them back like we were having a drinking contest. But we all seem to be on the same page as far as wanting the event to be the best it's ever been."

"That's great babe! But do you all have the same agenda?"

"What is that supposed to mean?"

"Well we both know why you decided to volunteer to plan this event. Why did they?"

"Why does that matter? It should only matter that we took the responsibility!"

"For now you're right that's all that matters, but just think about your main reason for taking this event head on wasn't for Pastor Coleman. You wanted to impress, better yet out do my mother. If they have a different set of motives, then who's to say they are going to come with the same intensity that you're bringing?"

"You don't think I thought of that? That's why I am the head planner in this event, I bring enough intensity for all of us. And whether your mother is impressed or not, this event will out do anything she has ever done at the church!"

"Okay Veronica just know what you're getting yourself into."

"Oh I do, believe me I do!"

Isaac left it alone, just happy his wife was happy, but he knew that the entire situation was a lose, lose. Especially for him, and even though Veronica didn't realize it yet for her too. Even if Veronica did manage to through the biggest and best party for Pastor Coleman. Mrs. Patton-Silver would still feel the need to compete and she absolutely refused to lose. Not taking much time to enjoy the heat from the water, Isaac was in and out of the shower. He was on a mission today, and had a great deal to get done before his day was done.

Mark made it to the job he absolutely hated a half hour early with a certain pep in his step. Quite different from his usual drab entrance, he was excited to be at work today and it definitely had nothing to do with the job. He wanted to get there early enough to see Roslyn before he started working. Just as he entered he was knocked off track by his line mate.

"Ho, ho, hold up, wait a minute Coleman is that you? Mr. Coleman what'chu doing here this early?"

"Good morning Mr. Williams."

"Umph Umph, naw young one don't Good Morning me! What you doing here all early? You usually come draggin in at the last minute."

"Whatever Mr. Williams! Traffic was light this morning."

"Yeah okay! Yo head is light this mornin'! It gotta be as open as yo nose is."

Mark felt his phone vibrating on his hip and cut conversation short with his older counter part, then headed for his assignment. Opening his phone he quickly read the text message inside.

"Are you gonna spend your whole mornin with that old pervert?"

Instantly looking around to see where she could be spying on him from unfortunately unable to spot her, Mark just kept forward on his journey. Before he could make it he received another text.

"So you not responding?"

He looked this time but kept walking. He quickly typed in his response, wondering what she wanted him to say, in response to spending time with the old man. Mark made it to the line just in time to see Roslyn walking into her office. He thought for a second about following her in but knew that it wasn't a good idea considering everyone in the plant would be talking about it. Especially after the spectacle that Mr. Williams had put on earlier. Instead Mark decided to stay put and continue there conversation through text.

"So what would you prefer me to do with my time?"

"ME!!!"

Pausing to come up with a cleaver come back for last statement, Mark stood for several seconds thinking. In all his cleverness all he seemed to scrounge up for a reply was "I'd like that." For all his talk and excitement Mark was far from a wordsmith. Roslyn was looking for a little verbal stimulation this morning, if only she knew she was searching in the wrong place.

"So is that all you wanted to show me last night?"

Once again Mark stumbled for seconds before replying.

"What else did you want to see?"

"Everything!"

Mark nearly turned red in the face, thinking of a reply this time he didn't have one at all. Lucky for him the horn sounded and line began shortly after. He was saved, at least until lunch time or until the line slowed down. Thinking to himself what would his reply be? What could he possibly say in response to that? The better question was would he actually show her everything?

Asia rolled over and looked at the clock, and all she could think was DAMN! She reached over pass the clock to her cell phone, pressing and holding the number three. Seconds later her secretary picked up.

"Good morning Mrs. Williamson, what can I do for you this morning?"

"Good morning Christine, do I have any meetings this morning?"

"No ma'am, you do have a 1:00 with Mr. Robinson and a 2:30 with Mr. Klein."

"Good, I won't be in until 1:00 so push Mr. Robinson back to 1:15 and Mr. Klein back to 2:45."

"No problem Mrs. Williamson I will get right on that."

"How many times do I have to tell you to just call me Asia. We do not have to be that formal."

"I do apologize Mrs. Will..... I mean Asia."

"Good, have a good morning and make sure you have those briefs on my desk for both clients."

"No problem Asia, see you this afternoon."

Asia immediately rolled out of bed and headed for the bathroom, she needed an aspirin. She couldn't even take a wild guess at how many glasses of wine she had the night before. Hell the better question was how the hell did she get home. All she knew was her head was banging, and screaming for some kind of relief. She opened the medicine cabinet and reached for the extra strength aspirin. Popping two in her mouth at once and with no water she swallowed them. Hoping they would kick in as quickly as possible. Coming back out of the bathroom after a quick brush of her teeth, she glanced at the clock again. Thinking to herself "Wow, he still not home?" Asia rarely noticed the time her husband came home anymore, because she was usually gone long before he made it home. It was already 9:30 and his shift ends at 7:00 he should've been home. Asia let her aching head get the best of her, she became overly concerned about her husband and his whereabouts. Just as her over active imagination had kicked in she heard the door open downstairs. Asia rushed back over to the bed and pretended to still be asleep. Listening as Terrance walked around the downstairs, finally she heard him approaching the stairs. As he reached the top of the stairs and then came into the bedroom he was startled by his wife laying in bed.

"Asia, Asia, AAAAsia What are you still doing here?"

"Huh, oh hey bay I decided to go in late today."

"Wow, you late something must be wrong. Are you sick or something?"

"No just thought I'd sleep in this morning is that okay with you?"

"Of course just surprising."

"So, Why are you just now getting home? It's almost ten o'clock?"

"Oh, I stopped by the gym this morning and then went and had breakfast."

Asia had more questions and even more suspicions, but decided it wasn't worth the trouble. She always wondered why Terrance's sex drive didn't match hers and at one point even considered he had another lover. She quickly let that notion go, who in their right mind would deal with his sexual inadequateness besides her. Terrance had questions of his own, for example why wasn't Asia at work. He was looking forward to coming home and relaxing, maybe even watching a movie or something. That was obviously not going to happen. Asia got out of the bed with intent, on going downstairs for something to drink and possibly making herself some breakfast. Terrance noticed the beauty who had just rose out of their bed, stopping his wife as she tried to get pass. Asia was easily in as good a shape as he was and didn't have to work as hard to stay that way. She ate whatever she wanted and never gained a pound. The form fitting night Tee more than did her justice, barely brushing against her shapely but firm ass. Terrance yanked his wife to him placing her directly in his chest. Throwing both arms around her, and squeezing tight. All the while looking down at her beauty allowing his hands to glide across her body. Starting right below the shirt line, just for the opportunity to feel her flesh. Doing a quick search for her panties, lucky for him she wasn't wearing any. Allowing his hands to venture back up to her hair and giving it slight tug to tilt her head back. Terrance took a taste of his wife's sweet lips, Asia was instantly turned on. Though she still wondered what had come over her husband. Spinning Asia around and bending her over the edge of the bed, there was no need for foreplay. Her excitement had already mounted as she stood bent over awaiting her husband's mass to over take her. Placing one hand on her lower back and using the other as guide into her depths, Terrance released a deep moan as he felt the warmth. The surprise of the encounter had still not warn off for Asia, heightening her senses and turning her on even more than the actual event. She wished this could be an all day event, but knew in the back of her mind it couldn't. Asia was in the moment, and as Terrance reached down lifting her cheeks up and spreading them apart Asia could feel all that he had to offer. It was just that simple, that was all she needed to concede. As she clutched the sheets, and buried her face into the mattress releasing a muffled moan. Wave after wave of her sweetness rushed over his manhood. Never missing a stroke it was only a matter of moments before he could no longer take it. Terrance had being a minute man down to a science, though today this was just what the doctor ordered. Between stress at work and the sexually frustration at home Asia climaxed easily today, and this was actually one of the few times she could say she was satisfied.

Chapter 9: *Fool's Paradise*

Amber woke up this morning as upset as when she went to sleep the night before. She was tired of taking the mental abuse from her husband, she wanted it to stop! The problem was she didn't know how to make it stop. She wasn't sure of her own power, or even if she had any. Sure she was a good mother and could clean when she wanted to, but what else could she really do. What made it even worse was that she felt as if she didn't have a strong woman in her life that she could turn to. Her mother was exceptive of the situation and said that it was the role of the woman to be her husband's release. Just as she started a trip through her mental rolodex the baby started crying and her day had officially started.

Amber's day consisted of cooking, cleaning, changing diapers, and thinking to herself. Mid-day is when it finally hit her "Asia and Veronica seem to have it all together." The question was can she actually ask them? Would it be reasonable? Could she air her and her husband's dirty laundry? After all Mark was the son of Pastor Coleman and an immediate reflection on him. Did she even have the right to discredit both of them at the same time. How did she know that her question wouldn't turn into church gossip and lead right back to her! Attempting to convince herself that this was a chance she couldn't afford to take. Amber decided against the move and went on about her day.

Veronica finally jumped out of bed with her day already planned. Her mind was still racing from this morning's conversation with her better half. She decided that a little morning workout would put her mind in a better place. Cardio always did the trick for Veronica, a half hour on the tread mill and she was up for anything the day might bring. It seemed as exercise gave her energy throughout the day. She headed for her closet and grabbed her shoes, then made a quick stop by her workout drawer. So she could grab a sports bra, and a pair of shorts after that she headed straight for the tread mill. Raising it to its highest setting it was as if she would be running up a mountain side. Unlike her husband's light jog, Veronica liked her pace to be that of an all out run. Endurance was the name of her game and she had the body to prove it. Not even three minutes into her warm-ups she already had sweat forming, so by the time she was midway through her run she was pouring with sweat. With her hair tied up in a scarf and a look of determination etched across her face. Veronica's body would've loved to give up in the last five minutes but her mind wouldn't think of it. Pushing herself to finish the run Veronica felt relieved when the machine finally started to move down into a normal stance. The treadmill slowed from the super hero's pace that she had it set to. In order to allow her to cool down for the last three minutes. Out of breath and muscles aching Veronica finished her workout and hit the shower.

She reached in and turned on the shower then, turned around and faced herself in the mirror. Excited by what she saw as the mirror began to fog, she decided to give herself a little show before her vision was completely blurred. Because of the immense amount of sweat, and the material that the workout gear was made of it was as if it formed a new layer of skin. Pulling it from her soaked body was a task in itself but the reward was worth it! Just before the mirror completely fogged Veronica was able to catch a glimpse of herself in full. Legs that would give any female track star a run for their money, and the midsection that rivaled that of most aerobics trainers. But her arms were the sexiest part, looking better than Angela Bassett's in Stella Got Her Grove Back. Veronica was a masterpiece, a thing of beauty she was a Goddess and deserved her own worshipers!

Speaking of which as Veronica finished her shower and began to lotion up. She noticed her phone had a couple missed calls and a text. She viewed the missed calls no voicemails, and both calls were blocked she knew what that meant. He was in town and there was no question as to what he wanted to do first. Veronica grinned her devilish grin, then quickly got dressed. It didn't take long to get completely dressed.

Especially considering the only thing she actually put on was a lavender panty and bra set that she had recently purchased at Victoria Secrets that perfectly matched the trench coat she had bought earlier in the year. Veronica decided to make a detour before visiting her out of town guest. Completing her ensemble with a pair of Lavender stilettos, she tied her coat and made for the garage.

Making a quick call to her out of town guest and explaining that she would be there in less than two hours. She quickly hung up the phone before she could hear the disappointment in his voice. Twenty minutes later she pulled up to her destination exiting the car and entering the offices she was immediately acknowledge by the receptionist.

"How are you today Mrs. Patton?"

"I'm fine Kim is my husband in his office?"

"Yes ma'am let me ring him and let him know you're here."

"No need! I'll surprise him myself."

Veronica headed for the stairs to her husbands office. As she reached the top and turned into the office she noticed another female employee that she didn't know hovering over her husband, with her cleavage pressed up and showing all too well. She was definitely flirting or had an interest, but her husband was not returning that interest. Veronica was sure of that because when she cleared her throat the young woman jumped in a startled manner while her husband sat cool, calm and collect.

"Hey Honey! What a surprise."

"Hello Dear, I thought it would be."

"Well it definitely is, to what do I owe this surprise?"

"Oh, nothing I was just in the neighborhood and thought I would stop by."

"Well I'm glad you did and looking so lovely. Oh yeah! How rude of me. This is Michelle, she's been with the company for the last couple months, and doing well I might add. Michelle, this is my wife Veronica."

"Hello Mrs. Patton!"

"Hello Michelle!"

"Michelle will you excuse my wife and I?"

"Of course Mr. Patton."

As Michelle left the room Veronica took in the full view of her husband's employee. Thinking to herself, Veronica deemed her to be little competition. She had a cute face, and a nice ass but the rest of her needed work in Veronica's opinion. She turned her attention to her husband as she closed the door to the office.

"Honey you left in such a hurry this morning I didn't even get a chance to see you off properly. Could you do me a favor?"

"Of course honey what is it?"

"Just wondering if you could call down and tell Kim that you don't want to be disturbed for about a half an hour?"

"Why is that honey is there something we need to discuss?"

"Something like that!"

Veronica untied the straps on her coat allowing the sides to come apart revealing her beautiful outfit underneath. Taking just a small glance Isaac picked up the phone, and called down to his secretary. Veronica walked over to her husband while he sat at his desk, moving his papers to make room for his wife, Veronica took a seat on the desk. Placing one of her legs between his, and allowing the other to just dangle off the desk. Isaac immediately grabbed his wife's leg gently caressing it, then leaning forward slightly he placed kisses from her knee cap to her thighs. As Veronica moaned with anticipation of where he might venture next. Knowing that this was one of those times that they were pressed for time, she raised her leg off the seat and placed her foot in Isaac's chest pushing him back. Allowing her coat to fall to the desk Veronica leaned forward and went directly for her husbands belt. Unbuckling then unzipping Veronica was on a mission. She was now standing in front of Isaac with hands on either side of his waist band attempting to wiggle him out of his pants. Isaac stood up, lifting his wife back up onto his desk as his pants fell around his ankles. Placing his lips on hers while she grabbed and pulled at his boxers. Finally releasing all of him, but only long enough to have him imprisoned once again. Though this time he was trapped inside her steamy moist walls. Veronica wasn't looking for her own enjoyment at least not right now. Her plan was solely based on his excitement, she wanted to surprise her husband and remind him that though she was his lady, she was also his freak! The excitement of the moment alone was enough to take Isaac to an instant climax. As Veronica threw back as much as her husband gave she could feel his eruption going off deep inside her walls as she had felt so many times before. Isaac heavy breathing in her ear was all she could hear until the moan of disappointment was released as well. Veronica realizing why her husband seemed bothered by his early arrival, took matters into her own hands. Leaning forward and whispering to him "I'll see you tonight Big Daddy!"

With that she removed herself from the desk and slipped her coat back on and was on her way. Putting her hands to her lips, then taking them away and blowing her husband a kiss.

Isaac sat there leaned back in his chair, thinking to himself how he had the best wife a man could possibly have. If only he had a clue! His wife came to see him, simply because it was on the way. She wasn't concerned with getting herself off because she was undoubtedly about to receive the royal service. The devil inside Veronica had taken over this day and she was on a mission of satisfaction. After leaving her husband's offices Veronica jumped on the expressway heading in the direction of Dearborn to the rendezvous she had planned earlier in the day. Arriving at the Hyatt Hotel across the street from the Fairlane Town Center with the same outfit that she had just seduced her husband in draped across her body. Veronica had work to do flipping her cell out of her purse she made the call. With nothing more than numbers uttered on the other end of the phone she had her final destination.

On her way up the elevator Veronica shared an elevator with a brother that looked identical to Detroit's ex-Mayor he stood about 6'4 with a thick build, he was looking quite debonair with his hair, a full beard kept thick and lined up nicely. Though she knew it couldn't be him. She was too busy to pay attention to him, as she was on a mission of her own at this time. She got off on her floor searching for her room number finally coming to the door. Without so much as a knock the door was slightly cracked so Veronica walked right in. Wasting no time or motion she untied her coat as she walked into the room. The man must've been waiting for her because he attacked her from behind roughly snatching the coat from her arms. He tossed it to the floor while holding Veronica tightly with one arm as he felt her up with the other hand. A rush came over her as he manhandled her, snatching her from her feet and carrying her to the couch in the living room. He tossed her face down into the couch pillows then propped her ass in the air removing the drenched lavender panties that by now had turned purple from her wetness. Palming each cheek the tall dark wonder knelt between them and tasted her sweetness. Lapping at her juices like a dog after the longest walk. He tasted Veronica as if he needed her fluids for survival. She buried her face deeper into the pillows because of the pure ecstasy that her chocolate lover was exposing her to. She knew she was wrong and nothing on this green earth could make her right but at this moment in time it didn't matter. All the facts were out the window. It didn't matter that she was married, and still had her ring on. It didn't matter that her husband adored her and she was his world. It didn't even matter that she had just finished allowing her husband to explore her body and leave every bit of himself in her. All that mattered at this moment was the flutter of his tongue and the way he was going to make her release. She clinched her muscles as her dark lover explored her depths. Just as Veronica was ready to explode, she felt nothing his tongue was gone. Removing her head from the pillow to look for him.

She noticed that he was still behind her without so much as a pair of boxer to cover himself he stood behind her with his large member in hand. Stunned by the vision of him Veronica stumbled over her words as she tried to speak. It was too late anyway as he stuffed all of himself into her. Her legs quivered and gave way as he slid about eight and a half inches of man flesh into her waiting paradise. The beauty of it all to her was he still had so much more to spare. Veronica was ready willing and able to take all that her Mandingo had to offer, and take it she would. He would proceed to give her every inch of himself for the next two hours without hesitation without remorse until she passed out from exhaustion and loss of fluids. Before she knew what happen Veronica was waking up inner thighs sticky from all the fun of the prior hours and stuck in a time warp. She had been out for at least two hours, and she was still tired. With only and hour and a half to get home and get ready before the ladies would again be at her house for the meeting. Her man of steel was still out cold, with no sign of movement. At least not anytime soon, she gathered her things and made for the door once again dressed in nothing more than her Lavender coat.

Veronica was a woman on a mission speeding through traffic with the hopes of making it home before company arrives. She still had to set up the conference room for the ladies, and Lord knew she needed a hot shower to get the smell of her morning off. Pulling up to the house and into the garage she jumped out rushing to the door. Once in the house she headed straight upstairs and jumped in the shower. She wouldn't have the luxury of taking her sweet time, after all she had guest arriving soon. Though the hot water felt marvelous on her aching body, it would only last for minutes and in this case it felt like seconds. Quickly in and out of the shower she threw on something presentable and headed down stairs. Straightening up what little there was to do, and pulling out her notes from yesterdays meeting. She was as ready as she was going to be, then it hit her. She needed to run to the cellar for today's assortment of wine. Quickly she grabbed four bottles and headed back upstairs. Just as she reached the top step the doorbell startled her. This time it was Amber who chose to be the early bird.

Mark went straight home after work no detours and not one stop off. As soon as he got home it was as if he was in a rush to get Amber out of the house. It was as if he was upset that she wasn't ready to go already. Looking at her in disbelief, as if to say I rushed home so you could be on time. Mark headed for the basement to get out of his work clothes. He hated smelling like the plant and since the baby was asleep he didn't have to make any stops. No kind words for his wife, the only thing he could think of was.

"I know you're not wearing that!"

Amber looked with contempt as she still wasn't over last night's debacle. So she rolled her eyes and kept it moving. She wasn't dressed yet but that still didn't give him the right to tear down the outfit she had spent the day in. Amber wasn't in the mood to be talked down to and figured she better leave before he has something else ignorant to say. She dressed quickly putting on a lovely sun dress that hid some of the extra curves of baby weight she had yet to lose. She still had the sex appeal but a make over wouldn't hurt at all. She had a natural beauty but could use a little help maintaining it. Nonetheless she looked good as she got ready to leave the house. Before she left she walked into her daughter's room and kissed her on the forehead and whispered.

"Mommy will be back soon."

Mark was done with his shower and now stood in front of the mirror with nothing more than a towel on. He stood with a confused look on his face as if he was attempting to make a decision. He picked up his phone and decided what the hell why not. Turning the bathroom into his own personal photo shoot Mark exposed his chest from four different angles. Then he lowered the towel allowing just a hint of his well manicured pubic hairs to show. Before taking the final picture with the towel around his ankles. Mark stored the pictures in his phone for later then proceeded to get dressed. Heading back upstairs just in time to see his wife leaving. In his head he was thinking wow, but out of his mouth spewed another sarcastic statement.

"That's better!"

Was the extent of his miserable attempt at a compliment, and was enough to make Amber slam the door behind her. Her intent was to wake the baby and she ended with much success. With an attitude Mark went and grabbed his precious daughter. His beautiful bundle of joy in one hand and cell phone in the other Mark rocked the little one back to sleep as he started sending his own personal picture show to Roslyn.

Asia was still on cloud nine after work, she had a wonderful morning and two great meetings this afternoon. What more could a woman ask for? She was in the mood to share the wealth of enjoyment. So before heading to the meeting she decided to stop by Kroger on her way and pick up some Margarita mix and a bottle of Tequila. This meeting would be twice as good as the last and she was going to make sure of it! Today was no different from any other with the exception of the explosion of the morning. Asia was still a speed demon and today she was in rare form dipping in and out of traffic on her way to Veronica's house. Arriving at her door in record time with goodies in hand, she was surprised to be the last one getting there but it didn't change much.

Veronica and Asia had a certain glow about themselves today and even seemed to have a energy boost. While Amber seemed to be in a world of her own. Veronica caught a glimpse of what was in Asia's bag and decided to do away with the wine glasses and broke out the blender. Amber who wasn't much of a drinker didn't seem to mind either way. The ladies weren't going to let their young friend ruin their sexual highs so they deemed her the taste tester. If the non drinker could stand to drink it, then it was a perfect mix. Needless to say they got a perfect mix on the first try, what they didn't know was Amber was in need of a drink today! So no matter what they concocted it was gonna be alright with her.

Three drinks in and Amber was starting to loosen up, she became a little more unwound with each sip. The ladies were feeling really good laughing and giggling and once again got a minimal amount of work done. The planning was easy, they all had their share of connections and could call in some favors especially Asia and Veronica. So getting to know each other was more important at least in the first couple of days. By the pouring of the fourth drink Amber had let the cat out of the bag.

"Ladies I think I am ready to either go back to work or back to school."

Both Asia and Veronica quieted down for just a second and let Amber speak. She went on about how she thinks the baby was old enough, and she had a pretty good support system between her mother and aunt so she wouldn't have to actually pay for a sitter. She went on and on for the next thirty minutes while the other two women sat there finally interrupting with the one question that she never went over.

"So what's the problem?"

"I don't think my husband will approve, or support the decision."

Both women looked in disbelief! Asia was the first to break the silence.

"Who cares what he wants! Yes y'all are married but you still have a life of your own and you have to live it! If he doesn't support you in your dreams how can he expect you to support him in his? Men!"

"Well let's not turn this into a male bashing campaign, because they're all not like that though a great deal of them are. You have some who support you every step of the way. Isaac has been my rock in every endeavor I have decided to take on. Well except when it comes to his mother! But that's another story!"

"You're right Veronica! Terrance is very supportive as well. He was there for me all through college and he is very understanding. As long as it doesn't interfere with his work."

"I wish Mark was the same way but he isn't and I don't want to go behind his back."

"Hell! Why not?"

"Asia stop it! You're right Amber you don't want to go behind his back. Talk to him first, but if he doesn't support you then you don't have a choice. You have to do what's best for you, and if he is too blind or doesn't care enough to consider that then to Hell with him. Then you go behind his back!"

All the ladies laughed and continued drinking and having a good time. Covering all topics from marriage to the church and in the process they even got some work done on the Pastor's event. Once again the time flew by and the ladies were stuck wondering where it all went.

Mark's night was going beautifully a continuous picture exchange between he and Roslyn made it that way. Mark had already put the baby down for the night and it was just him and Roslyn sending messages back and forth for the afternoon and most of the evening. Their curiosity for each other was at an all time high, and something had to be done about it. Their over active imaginations had them sexually frustrated. Mainly because he was stuck with the baby tonight, and she had to be to the hospital in the morning. Mark wished there was a way for him to sneak out and fulfill all his desires for the night but there wasn't and just as he was ready to hit the peek of his sexual heights he heard the close of a car door. Looking out of the back window he noticed his wife walking with a certain stagger in her step. There was absolutely no way that Amber was what it appeared she was. Was there?

Mark walked from the back room to meet her in the kitchen as she finally made it through the back door. She stood there fumbling with the keys, long enough to be mugged three times over. Amber looked up with the meanest scowl he had ever seen from her.

"You didn't hear me pull up, Mark? You could've come a got the door!"

"Why would I do that? That's why you have keys!"

"So what! Does that mean you can't open the door? I know I got keys! You ain't telling me nothing, Hell I live here why wouldn't I have keys!"

"Amber you've been drinking!"

"You damn right Mr. Man and not only have I been drinking but dammit. I'm drunk!"

"Amber you need to calm down, and lower your voice. The baby is sleeping."

"Don't tell me what to do! I'm tired of you always telling me what to do. Let me tell you something I do what I wanna do! Matter of fact I do what's best for me!"

"What the Hell are you talking about. Maybe you should go and lay down and sleep some of the liquor off."

"I just told you! I am gone do what I want to do!"

"Whatever Amber I'm going to bed!"

"Yeah you do that then!"

Mark turned around and walked out of the kitchen and through the living room making it to their bedroom and closing the door. Amber felt good about herself she had made her point but knew it really didn't mean too much considering it was the liquid courage not her doing most of the talking. On top of that Mark had dismissed her lecture as rants of a drunk. Amber was a bit too tipsy to be ready for bed just yet and a lot too horny as well. She walked into the bathroom and turned on the shower. Stripping down into nothing quickly hoping the water would sober her up a bit, but not too much because she would have to still be a little inebriated to do what she intended on doing. The shower was a little something to take the edge off, and of course take the smell of alcohol off as well. The shower was quick not nearly long enough to enjoy, but Amber had her own thoughts of pleasure this night. Walking into their bedroom were Mark laid half asleep she made use of the dimmer on the light switch as she entered. She wanted her husband to see the peace offering she had in mind. Inching closer to her husband as he lay there like unsuspecting prey for a hunter. Though Amber could be considered a bit of a prude, the alcohol took away any of the inhibitions she might have had on this night. Uncovering her husband as she broke his slumber, Mark was startled by what happen next. With no warning Amber engulfed every inch of Mark's thickness and stroked him with her mouth as if she was a professional. Mark was immediately as awake as he or his friend down below had ever been. Opening his eyes to a vision of his beautiful wife's naked body and head bobbing as if it was Halloween and he was a barrel of apples. Mark was instantly turned on, but still had to wonder what could have possibly gotten into his wife. She was working better than any of the women he had paid so much attention to in the videos he had watched in cyberspace. Mark marveled as Amber worked him as he never thought possible. She had the perfect formula that had him ready willing, and waiting on the opportunity to please her as much as she was pleasing him. Running his fingers through her hair as a sign of enjoyment. As if she couldn't already tell she was doing a wonderful job from all the panting and moaning she had a grown man doing. She knew it was almost over when he reached down with his free hand to grab the other side of her hair as well. Making sure to tease him just long enough, then pulling her mouth away to make sure he doesn't blow his load before she is satisfied as well. Pulling away from him, forcing him to let go of her hair was a task but one she was up for. She moved back and looked up at Mark smiling. Enjoying the view of his wife body as if it was for the first time Mark leaned over grabbing the handful of breast that she had. Leaning even further over he took one into his mouth suck savagely until her nipple stiffened. It didn't take much to turn Amber on, she had so much time learning what pleased her husband that she didn't know her own body that well. She was happy with the basics, and then as much penetration as he could offer. Mark was one of two men who had ever touched Amber and considering he wasn't bad in bed made him the best she had experienced by default. The truth was whether Mark was bad or excellent in bed Amber wasn't capable of telling, all she truly knew was she liked it. Mark knew she did as well so he gave his wife exactly what she was yearning for. Pushing her gently onto her back and following right behind, roughly kissing her neck while giving her the missionary sex that her body desired. Catching a very romantic rhythm, as if he could hear Luther Vandross singing in the background. He stroked his wife as listened to the lyrics in his head.

"Let me hold you tight, if only for one night. Let me keep you near to easy away your fears. It would be so nice if only for one night."

Mark allowed that mental beat to dictate his stroke, until he buried his face in his wife's shoulder and lost her mental picture. Just that quickly she had been replaced by the pictures he had enjoyed so much before his wife arrived. The mere thought of Roslyn was enough to change his entire sexual theme. She was more up beat and his thoughts of her had nothing at all to do with love, and everything to do with sex! His pace quickened moving from the smooth tunes of Luther, to the bass pounding of R. Kelly. At this moment with thoughts of Roslyn dancing through his head Mark didn't see nothing wrong wit a little "Bump and Grind." The faster pace and harder stroke was a bit of a surprise for Amber, but a pleasant one in her intoxicated state. She enjoyed feeling every inch of him ravage her innocence, making her feel like less of a little girl and more like a woman. She wasn't sure what had come over her but she loved the feeling. So much in fact that she indulged a bit more, letting out a slight moan. That moan grew more intense the deeper and harder Mark went. As he lost himself in a sexual day dream. Introducing his wife to a threesome that she was unaware of. Luckily for her she didn't know, because that would've ruined her transient to another plain, as her moans turned into words, and her words into phrases, and her phrases into sentences.

"Mmmmmmmmm"

"Yes!"

"Yes, baby!!"

"Yes, baby! Give it to me just like that."

It wasn't until Mark hit the bottom, that the two of them sexually intertwined. As he spread her legs as wide as they could go, and dipped himself completely into her depths. Then gave her a circular grind, Amber lost what little mind she had left and the words that followed were the ones that usually brought every man to his peak.

"FUCK ME!"

It was too bad Mark was in a trance, because he wasn't able to give his wife her just do. She had stepped completely out of her shell tonight, with the help of a little liquid courage. But he was so wrapped up in another woman that he barely even noticed. As they both lay there afterwards satisfied beyond what either of them had ever experienced with one another before. Luckily for Amber she didn't have the ability to read minds. Because while he was the only thing on hers, she was the furthest thing from his.

Chapter 10: *Fantasy Fulfilled*

It was another long night at the hospital for Terrance and he couldn't wait to get home. Hell if he was lucky Asia called in late again, and maybe he could bend her over one more time. At least that was the thought that ran through his head as he prepared to leave for the day. Gathering all his things he decided that it was just about time to leave. As he started his mad dash for the door, he was interrupted by her beauty. It was the same nurse, or better yet soon to be nurse that had caught his attention before. This time however she was alone. Which made it a perfect time for a proper introduction. Terrance walked by as she sat trying to understand the text from which she read. Unable to help himself Terrance struck up conversation, or at least attempted as such.

"That doesn't look like any medical book I've ever read."

"Well some women swear by Cosmo's healthy living section. You should check it out sometime."

They both shared in a light chuckle. As Terrance stopped to chat for a while before he left the hospital.

"So I see you're a bit early for your shift today."

"You know what they say! Early bird gets the worm."

"Yeah, that is what they tend to say isn't it. I don't think we've met formally. My name is Dr. Williamson, but everyone just calls me Terrance. Or at least the people who know me around here."

"Well in that case Dr. Williamson, my name is Roslyn and yes I'm a little early today. I've been told that it's a necessity around these parts."

"I see you have been getting pretty good information from our staff then. What else have they told you?"

"Well a couple of the nurses told me to be careful around the doctor's in this building because they are only out for one thing."

"Is that right? Well in that case be sure to believe half of what you see, and none of what you hear. That is of course unless you hear it from me."

"I will keep that in mind sir."

"You do that Roslyn, you do just that. I hope you have an enjoyable day, and that you learn a lot."

"You do the same Terrance."

With that Terrance continued on with the end of his work day. As he looked forward to being off for the next couple days for the yearly get away that he and Asia usually enjoyed this time of year. They enjoyed this trip no matter what conflicts their respective schedules provided. It was finally time for Terrance to break loose from his constraints for a while. This was the only time he could be this free, every year the couple would have a new adventure. This trip was probably the only thing keeping their relationship together.

Mark woke the next morning after a wild night with his wife. He seemed refreshed and renewed, he was ready for anything or so it seemed. Nothing seemed different about today he quickly dressed and rushed off to work. Looking forward to seeing the woman that made his day and night yesterday, unfortunately realizing mid-drive that this was one of those days that Roslyn had off because of school. It was as if the air was sucked right out of him. No longer excited about the work day and just like that the pep that had been in his step was gone. It also hit him that it was another full day of him listening to the old man, another part of the day he truly wasn't looking forward to.

Snatching his phone from his hip, he sent a quick text message to Roslyn. Gonna miss you today, how about we do a late lunch? Putting his phone back on his hip not expecting much after that, he continued on his road to work. Ready for an exhausting day. Sure enough as soon as he arrived the loud mouth old man was there and started right up.

"Didn't expect to see you today! Thought since ya boss took off, you would've done the same."

"Why would I do something like that?"

"Well since she has a thing for you and it's obvious now that you have one for her too. Thought y'all might be clearing the air today: If you know what I mean."

"Listen there is nothing going on with me and her, I am a married man and she's my boss. Be serious!"

"You always know someone is lying when they start tossing out facts that have nothing to do with what you're talking about right then. Hey if that's your story by all means stick to it."

"Yeah okay Mr. Williams! Am I gonna have to carry you as usual today or are you gonna actually do some work?"

"Boy I was working in this plant while you was at home still stinken up diapers. I've done more work in a day then yo ass has done all year. I was here before all these fancy machines they got doing the job now so if you gotta carry me it's only because this company knows they owe me."

"The company might but I don't! What was that you said about facts?"

"Boy this young generation is a lazy bunch of good for nothings."

Mark knew that this was going to be a long day, but luckily for him his phone was vibrating. Looking down he saw the message that would make this long day seem well worth it. A smile quickly came across his face, but soon evaporated when he heard the voice of his old co-worker behind him. "I take it that's your wife making you smile" The text from Roslyn had made Mark's morning, now all that was left to do was come up with an excuse for Amber. He knew just what to say to her too, he would call her at lunch time and let his wife know that he would be working a double today. So she would have to take the baby to her mother's house. Today was going to be special, he and Roslyn had been playing phone games taunting and flirting with each other and for the first time they would actually be alone together. Only catch was he didn't get to go home before their date, and that was going to be a problem.

They say time flies when you're having fun, but it's quite the opposite when you're hoping to have fun. The day seemed to drag on forever, as if each minute was an hour. Mark would work for what seemed like two hours, and notice that only ten minutes had passed. He was unbelievably impatient, he wanted so badly for his work day to end but it just didn't seem as if it ever would. That was until the clock finally struck 3:00. Mark rushed out of the plant like a man on a mission, not even wasting time with texting he immediately called Roslyn to find out where she was. Telling him her address and directions to get there, she hung up the phone and waited for his arrival.

By the time Mark got off the phone he was a bit nervous, he made a just in case stop at the gas station for a box of condoms. After all he was always taught better safe than sorry! It was a half hour later when he pulled up to the front gate of her condo. The Southfield community, was a mix village with condos and apartments mixed in together. She must've been anticipating his arrival because without even asking when he called back she buzzed the gate to let his vehicle in. Giving him directions to get to her part of the community, before long Mark was parking in her drive-way. Getting out of the car still in his work attire, she had the door open as he walked up the path. Throwing her arms around him as she greeted him walking in the door. A bit surprised by the greeting Mark returned the hug, and smiled. Both of them were happy to see each other. Though Mark was the first to acknowledged that fact.

"So.... Missed you at work today."

"Is that so Mr. Coleman, well with that said I missed being at work today."

With that slight exchange Mark was quiet again, thinking to himself. "What in the world am I doing here?" With another look at the beautiful woman that stood before him he had the answer he was looking for. He was there for her, and whatever she may be offering this night. Nothing else flowed through his mind at that time. Not his wife, not his child, and definitely not what his father would think of him. He was living in the moment, and at that very second, he could think of nothing else but Roslyn!

Roslyn knew exactly what she wanted even if Mark was still unsure. She had flirted and played long enough, now she wanted to see in person what she had the pleasure of seeing over the phone. Looking over him as if she was a Lioness, and he was her prey. She had hunted for him, and now she had him cornered and it was time to pounce. Leading him into the living room she sat him down on the couch and asked if he would like something to drink or something to snack on. Mark's mouth watered at the thought of snacking on her, but he managed to control his thoughts. Instead he only requested a glass of water to quench his thirst.

"Are you sure you wouldn't like something a little stronger?"

"What did you have in mind?"

"I use to be a bartender, I could whip you up something real quick. If you like?"

"It's a bit early for alcoholic beverages don't you think?"

The Congregation

"Anytime after 12:00pm Monday thru Saturday and you are well within' your rights to have a drink."

They both laughed for a second but in the end Mark decided he would rather stay sober. He wanted to remember every waking moment of this afternoon, and didn't want it tainted by an alcoholic moment. Though it may have been in his good senses to have at least one drink to loosen him up a bit. He was even sitting on the couch stiff at this point. As she returned with Mark's bottled water, she insisted that he make himself comfortable. To which Mark responded quickly.

"In that case do you mind if I use your restroom, and had a face towel? I feel a little sweaty and just want to wash my face off."

"Of course not here, I'll do you one better come with me."

Roslyn led him down the hallway and up the stairs to the master bedroom. Handing him a face towel and drying towel she showed him into her personal bathroom.

"Here you can use my shower, I told you to make yourself comfortable. If you like I will wait for you downstairs."

"There's no need for that, thank you for letting me use the shower I can really use one after today."

"It was that hard at work without me?"

Once again the two of them laughed, as Mark prepared for his shower. Roslyn left the bathroom but didn't venture too far waiting just outside the bathroom doorway. Mark started to close the door but thought better of it, hell he wanted her to see just what he had in store. Stripping off his shirt, then reaching into the shower and turning the water on full blast. Mark decided to let the water heat up while he finished undressing. While Roslyn pretended not to watch through the bathroom mirror which she could easily see from the way her bed was set up in her room. Folding his pants and tossing them on the vanity stool in the bathroom. Mark had totally forgot about the three pack of condoms he had just purchased from the store. As he got in the shower closing the door behind him and enjoy the warmth of the water his purchase fell from his pants pocket onto the bathroom floor. Roslyn immediately noticed the condoms, and came into the bathroom to take a closer look. She blushed thinking to herself "Oh he just knew he was getting some huh?" for a split second she thought about not letting him have any today. But when she turned and saw his silhouette through the stain glass shower door. She easily allowed that thought to melt away. She wasn't however going to let condoms go unnoticed, swinging open the shower door letting all the steam escape and a whiff of cold air come through. She examined his body with her eyes, and became envious of the soap suds that had the pleasure of touching his nakedness when she did not.

"So are you gonna close the door so I can rinse off?"

"Well that depends on how you answer my question?"

"And what question would that be?"

"What were you planning on doing once you got out of the shower?"

"I was going to...........umm, well I was gonna."

"Come on don't be shy! You are gonna freeze to death if I don't close this door. I know you feel the chill."

"I mean I was going to, well you know. I......."

"Well here how about I help you out. Look over my shoulder at the floor."

Mark peeked his head out of the shower and looked over her shoulder noticing the unmoved pack of condoms on the floor. Then with a look of embarrassment on his face he turned back to Roslyn trying to put the words together. Before he could get another word out Roslyn turned and walked out of the bathroom.

"Roslyn wait. I can explain."

"Make sure you rinse off before you come out here and dry of too I don't want you tracking water and suds all through my house."

Mark jumped back under the now luke warm water and rinsed all the suds off his body. Jumping out of the shower and patting himself dry then throwing the towel around his waist as quick as he possibly could. Rushing into the bedroom to find Roslyn waiting naked on the bed with herself fully exposed.

"Make sure you bring your package with you!"

Mark's jaw dropped as he stood in the doorway between the bathroom and the bedroom with his mouth open wide.

"Now all you have to do is stick your tongue out and put that mouth to good use."

Without so much as a second thought Mark knelt and picked up the box of condoms. Then stood up and walked to the bed, and tried something he had never even experienced with his wife. He tasted for the first time the sweetest nectar in the world, with someone he barely knew. Lapping at her like a thirsty dog, until she eased him with her words. Explaining that she wasn't going anywhere and he could eat his fill. Slowing himself and taking the time to actually enjoy her flavor Mark was intoxicated by her taste. Exploring her depths with his lips and tongue he insisted on capturing her scent in the hairs of beard and mustache. So that even after his taste testing was done he could still indulge in her scent long after. Roslyn allowed him to taste her until she could barely wait anymore. She insisted that he take her, she wanted to feel the parts of him that she had only seen thus far. Mark obliged and quickly reached for the box that he had placed by her thigh. Ripping open the package and shoving his fingers into the box pulling out all three wrappers. Tearing open one of the packs with one of his hands and his teeth, while reaching down with his free hand grabbing his already swollen member. Rolling his protection over himself without a problem only moments had passed between the actions. He positioned himself between her legs pulling her to the edge of the bed and inserting his lower head. As Roslyn exhaled and allowed him to separate her lips with his manhood. Mark slid himself deep inside her over and over allowing her juices to lubricate his movements. With each and every stroke Roslyn went wild. Finally clawing, and digging her nail less fingertips into his back. It was no time at all before she was overtaken by her first climax with Mark. Enjoying every drip of her eruption Mark continued his precision, protected in more than one way by the thin layer between them. The condom allowed Mark to last longer than he normally would without one and he planned on taken full advantage of that. Making sure his boss was fully satisfied in that position before moving on to the next. Mark gave her the pleasure that she had only dreamed about thus far. Forcing her to remember that this was only the beginning. Wait until they actually got familiar with each other.

As Mark enjoyed his hours away from home Amber was preparing for the last meeting of the week with the ladies. Amber was in route to dropping off the baby at her mother's house so that she could make it on time. When she received a call informing her that her mom had an emergency and wouldn't be able to keep the baby. Instead of pitching a fit she decided that she would just go back home instead. Amber called Veronica to let her know that she wouldn't be able to make it tonight. Much to the dismay of the ladies, they were very understanding. They hung up with each other and before long Amber was back in the comfort of her home. With nothing to do and a baby who had been rocked to sleep by the car Amber was free to do nothing.

Seconds after getting off the phone with Amber, Veronica heard the door bell ring and found Asia at the front door. Explaining the situation for today's meeting Asia instantly felt the same disappointment as the rest of the ladies. In just a short time together each of the ladies had begun to look forward to the time that they shared. They weren't just working on a project together, nor were they just church members. They had become friends, the type of friends that were there for each other. So instead of having a twosome if the third party couldn't make it to the meeting Veronica, and Asia decided to take the meeting to her. With a quick phone call and three bottles of wine in hand the ladies mounted up in their respective cars and made their way to Amber's house. Well that was after a quick call to her cell to get directions and to let her know they were coming. The meeting was saved and the ladies got a great deal of planning done, mainly because they were limited to only three bottles of wine of which they only emptied two.

This had been an extremely long week for all parties involved, and next week was going to be that much longer it seemed. Nothing would settle everyone down more than the upcoming event, and with planning almost complete the congregation had so much to look forward to. Towards the end of the meeting the ladies decided that the next meeting should be held at the actual event location. That way they could get a true estimate of the building location and how everything would look when it was finally set up.

Chapter 11: *Girl Talk*

"So ladies the date is coming up really soon, we have the guest speaker, as well as the special invited guest. We need to celebrate a job well done. Maybe a night on the town for just the ladies considering we did all the work with our "oh so busy husbands" doing much of nothing throughout the process. What do you ladies think maybe go out for a night on the town?"

"A night on the town Veronica? I would've never guessed you to be the type to be hanging out in the world."

"Wow! I wouldn't have guessed that one either Amber but you know what they say never judge a book by its cover."

"How right you are Asia you could not even begin to judge this book by the cover. You would have to get all up in these pages. The surprises are plentiful! As far as going out goes it's just hanging out Amber it's not like I said we should spend the night at Watt's or Henry's Palace."

Veronica and Asia both laughed out loud as Amber softly snickered so that she did not let on to the fact that she had never been to either place and only heard about the goings on at the two places. It took all of two seconds and the look of innocence in Amber's eyes for Veronica to realize that Amber had no clue as to what really went on in those two special places. With a quick nudge to Asia to get her attention Veronica drew it back to Amber.

"Amber have you ever been to either of those clubs?"

"You can't see it in her eyes Asia? She might've heard of them but she has not even been on Fenkell. She looks like she's been in church her entire life. Hell she can't be more than 22 years old she just getting used to being legal."

"Um I'd appreciate it if you guys wouldn't talk about me like I'm not right here. To be honest I have never been to either place, but never really had an interest in going. Doesn't excite me too much."

"Doesn't excite you? Wow everything about a man excites me from the way they walk to the way they talk. Hell I even love the way they smell."

"That's not too hard to believe when you have a man as fine as Terrance it can't be too hard to love men! I hope you don't get offended by this but your husband is fine! But you probably hear that all the time."

"Yeah I do but what was it we were just saying about books and covers?"

They both stopped midway through their sips and placed their wine glasses on the table. Considering the women were halfway through their second bottle of Merlot. Both women stopped and looked in amazement with Veronica being the first to speak. Attempting to ensure that there were no hard feelings by her words she attempted to clean up her comments.

"Well I was just saying Asia that all of us have very attractive mates but your man could very well be a model or something."

"Yeah I have noticed that he is a very attractive man as well."

Amber chimed in attempting to cut what they both thought was tension in the air. Truth was Asia had heard these facts so many times that the thought of it all never bothered her anymore. She was more than comfortable with women finding her man attractive after all if no one else found him attractive why would she. No one wants someone that no one else wants. Though if they only knew that looks weren't everything, Asia would have happily traded the great looks for some great sex at this point the lonely nights of touching herself were becoming oh so tiring.

"Well you know what they say everything that glitters ain't gold."

"Ain't that the truth!"

"Wow listen to little Amber, she said that with so much conviction. Is the love life of the young couple going south?"

"Can't be they are in their twenties he probably can't get enough! I remember when I was in my twenties my man couldn't get enough. Hell he was ready when I was awake, when I was sleep. Hell even when I wasn't ready his ass was. Probably why it didn't last."

"I can remember those days!"

"Well I'm glad you all can remember your hay days because at this point I can't get Mark away from the damn internet long enough to actually touch me. Hell he spends so much time touching himself while watching that pornography on the internet and those nasty DVD's he brings home every night."

"You let him watch all that by his self? You don't join him?"

"Join him of course not! I don't watch things like that!"

Veronica and Asia laughed again at the expense of Amber's innocence. They couldn't help but reminisce on their innocent days once again. Chattering back and forth about how they could remember when they thought porn was vile and filthy. Even though Asia came into her own much later than in Veronica's case. They could still find some common ground to chuckle about Amber's situation. Amber still didn't find any humor in the situation.

"So what do you use to play with yourself? Don't tell me that's something you don't do either?"

"I DON'T DO THAT!"

"Wow! With your generation being as free willed and wild as y'all are I would've thought I would be the one learning from this conversation but I see I definitely have you beat! Hell ever since I found out that the good looks of the good doctor don't transcend into the bedroom I only had two choices. Either find a suitable bedroom replacement on the side or get to know myself extremely well. Luckily, I decided to try my HAND at the latter."

"Are you saying that that gorgeous hunk of man that you have doesn't get the job done in the bedroom?"

"No what I'm saying to you two is that beautiful man couldn't get the job started even with an instruction manual."

They both stood in amazement as if they had just witnessed a black candidate win the presidential race. Their mouths dropped open as if her words had the ultimate shock value. With disbelief written all over their faces, Veronica attempted to bring herself and Amber back down to earth. The conversation continued with both women stuck with a totally different out look on Terrance and his unbelievable looks. The looks weren't as good anymore, he couldn't be viewed as a sex symbol anymore. At least not since they knew that he wasn't capable of fulfilling that fantasy. The ladies kept the conversation going allowing the wine to take it's toll. Releasing secrets that most of their closest friends hadn't gotten wind of. By the end of the night the plan was complete they would be hanging out tomorrow night and enjoy a ladies night out on the town.

"So ladies are we telling the gentlemen our plans or are we just going to let them believe that we will be working on the event one more night?"

"Terrance doesn't know if I'm coming or going. So I don't have to explain anything."

"Isaac won't have a problem with it either, so that just leaves you Amber."

"Well if it's not about church then I should be at home taking care of the baby, or at least that's the way Mark thinks it should work. I don't have time off so I guess I have to stick with the event theme."

"Then it's settled one day next week is "Girls Night Out!" Hell we've all worked hard and we deserve it."

With that the women all finished with their drinks then all set out to make their way home.

Chapter 12: *A Long Drive Home*

The long drive inspired Amber to think about her situation at home. How is it Mark can have all the fun in the world, and she's stuck at home sexually frustrated taking care of their beautiful baby on a regular basis. True enough she had gained a pound or two since their marriage but she had never been a size 2 in her life. She was far from being a cow as well. She still had a shape unlike a lot of women she had seen while out and about grocery shopping. Her point was simple she wasn't bad looking enough to be stuck with this situation. She was still attractive and she was going to prove it to herself. Pulling into the driveway her mind was set. Tomorrow night she was going to dress to kill and where ever the ladies started their night she was going to flirt with whomever she pleased. Just harmless flirting, she didn't plan to be forward but she wasn't planning to shy away from attention. She still had men who went out of their way to give her compliments and attention. So this would be her night to enjoy that attention and those compliments.

As she exited the car that she had pulled up into the backyard she noticed Mark hadn't even left the light on in the back. This made her even more upset, I can't see anything back here, what if someone was back here waiting on me? Hell he wouldn't even care, his ass probably in the basement having a wild jack session before it's time for him to go to work. She finally played with the back door long enough to make it in the house. She walked in and went straight to the bedroom to find that the bed was empty and so was the babies crib. Knowing that he didn't have the baby downstairs while he enjoyed himself she became even more upset. Pulling off her coat and dropping it on the floor of the room she rushed to the basement stairs nearly trippin on her way down. She could see him but not the baby as he sat in front of the computer.

"Mark!!!"

"What?"

"Mark! Where is the baby?"

"Doesn't seem like you care too much, considering you're just getting home. Now does it?"

"You know I had to go and meet with the ladies of the church for the event."

"You just getting home from that? You knew I had to go to work too didn't you?"

"You don't have to be there until 10:00 and it's only 8:30. What are you talking about?"

"Well I didn't know if you were going to make it back in time so I took the baby around to my mother's house."

"Why would you do that this early? You don't usually leave the house until 9:30."

"Wasn't sure you would make it. My mother wanted to see the baby anyway, but you better go get her now she's been down there for a while and Mom has to work in the morning."

"So you can't go get her before you go to work?"

"No I need to relax before going to that damn job so you'll have to do it."

Amber was furious as she ventured back up the stairs and to the bedroom to grab her coat and keys to pick up Lauren from her grandmother's house. Mark never even took the time to look up and acknowledge her presence in the doorway as he told her to go get the baby. His eyes were glued to the words on the computer screen as he instant messaged a young woman from the internet.

Asia's drive home wasn't as irritating but just as uneventful. All the talk about masturbation had her engine running a mile a minute and the beautiful melody of Raheem DeVaughn and Floetry didn't help her endeavor. She was on tilt before even pulling up to her door listening to all the things that could possibly be done to her as the artist sang back and forth. She was in total agreement she was in the mood for a marathon work out. She pulled up to her lavish home on Detroit's Westside more than ready to release her wild side. Hitting the button for the garage she pulled in then hurried up the well lit walkway from the garage to the back door. The porch light was on and she could here CNN news playing as she opened the back door which was already unlocked. She was in luck this was one of the rare nights that her husband was still home. Maybe she would be getting off with his help tonight. She dropped her bags directly behind his T.V. chair leaning over the back of the chair giving him a full kiss on the lips acquiring his full attention. Walking around the chair while their lips were still locked pushing him down into the chair then straddling him as he sat. Asia hiked her skirt up to her waist as their passionate kiss added to her wetness. She readied herself for an unbelievable night of passion it seriously must have slipped her mind who she was married too. Either that or the liquor had taken a serious effect. Just as she reached down to remove her panties and help him unbutton his pants. The kiss broke, and the unbelievable words eked from his lips. At the same time the news anchor spoke the words he had been waiting for the entire night.

"Tonight we discuss the importance of Medicaid and why there are still hospitals who don't accept it as medical coverage."

"Babe I've been waiting for this report all night give me a second will you please."

Amazed by the comment Asia stopped in her tracks removing herself from her current position. With a serious look of disappointment written all over her face, she grabbed her bag then made her way up the stairs for another lonely night of pleasuring herself.

"Wow!" Asia thought to herself mainly because, her sexual advances had been turned down yet again. This time for something as trivial as the damn news, Asia was forced up the stairs to question what the hell was really going on. Gazing into the mirror she decided it couldn't be her, and it had been going on since the beginning so that excluded the possibility of another woman. Besides who in their right mind would cheat on her. She took another look into the mirror and smiled, thinking to herself the truth was even if they did get it on downstairs the end result would have been the same. Terrance had not satisfied her in years, and the times he had she could count on one hand. Even those times he didn't seem like himself as if someone or something had possessed his body taking his love making limits to new heights. Standing there she pondered what it would be like to be with someone else. Flashes of other men darted through her mind. Starting with movie stars, and entertainers, moving on to professional athletes. Though this wasn't her first time with these thoughts tonight the famous hook just wasn't going to do the job. She made the thoughts more personal, made the men regular. Men she dealt with on a day to day. Standing in the mirror, with thoughts of the new teller the bank had just hired earlier in the week. Just as her fantasy began to get interesting everything came to a screeching halt. Her thoughts were interrupted by the irritating ring of their home phone. She assumed it would be answered almost immediately by her news watching husband. When that didn't quite workout, she reluctantly eased across the master bedroom and answered the phone.

"Hello!"

She said with a certain disgust in her voice. But the tone quickly disappeared once she heard the voice on the other end of the phone.

"Hey Auntie! How are you today?"

"Christopher is this you?"

"Your favorite nephew! How are you this evening?"

"If you only knew. I'll be fine were you calling for your Uncle? He's downstairs watching the news."

"Yeah I guess I am calling for him. He left me a message about some dinner event that's gonna cost me $50.00 a plate. Any idea what this is about?"

"Yes we are throwing a dinner event for our pastor and he was inviting you I believe as one of the guest speakers for the event. But let me get him for you because I don't want to give you any incorrect information."

"Is that right? Why me? He knows I'm not a fan of church, period. No problem though anything for my favorite aunt and uncle."

"Favorite huh? Well let me get him for you."

As she walked to the stairs her mind began to wander once again but this time it didn't make it all the way back to the bank teller. She was even closer to home this time. Though she had known him since he was just a boy, her nephew by marriage had grown into a fine chocolate man. Not only did he have his family's exceptional looks, but unlike his uncle it was evident that he actually took advantage of his physical abilities. After insuring that her husband picked up the phone she allowed her mind to wander even more. Though she never let on, she had secretly wondered about Christopher for a couple years now. Every time he stops by or comes over for a holiday it's always a different woman and each time they appear to be totally different from the last. One thing always remains the same though they are always very attractive and always seem to be all into him. What was it that kept these women fawning over Chris? He had recently found success in his new occupation, but it couldn't be that because he had just started to blow up as a journalist of the paper this year. Before that he was a teacher for a short period of time, and still before that he was just a student with odd jobs. The only thing that could possibly be keeping these women interested even for a short time had to be below the waste. Her imagination took over allowing her body to overheat at the thought of her next of kin. As her hands began to caress her own full breast she imagined the rough hands of a man. Reaching new heights with each touch her heart raced, and lips quivered at the mere through of Christopher's lips enjoying the nape of her neck. Her hands traveled lower to enjoy the intense wetness that she had to offer. A quick thought ran through her mind, her husband had no idea what he was missing out on this night. She felt like letting herself go tonight, and wanted to let every bit of the freak inside her out to play. Unfortunately it would happen in her mind and with only herself to play with, she would again be left unfulfilled.

Veronica had a totally different and much more eventful trip home. Unlike the other two couples Veronica and her husband had moved outside the city limits so her drive would take her a bit further. Unfortunately that trip was a bit more dangerous considering her lightly intoxicated state. Combine that with the lead foot she had inherited from a father she barely knew it was enough to get her in a bind she wasn't going to easily get out of. As she sped up to make a quickly changing yellow light, she couldn't help but notice a police car sitting in a parking lot waiting for a speeding vehicle just like hers. Removing her foot from the gas pedal, but being sure not to attach it to the brake just yet, Veronica allowed the car to slow down. Though it was too late because no sooner than her car was slowing down, she noticed the officer's car pull out in pursuit.

"Damn!"

She exclaimed knowing what was coming next. Just as she thought the blue and white lights started flashing and the sirens rung loud. Quickly looking down at the speedometer she realized her lead foot had got her in trouble again. Pulling over to the side of the road, and immediately going on a search through her glove box for all the important materials that the officer would be asking for. At the same time keeping one eye glued to the rear view mirror. Even with the dim lit evening that she was so trying to enjoy she noticed the frame of the man in uniform approaching her car. Her search was quickly halted by a tap on the driver side window. She leaned back over to her side of the car and hit the button for the window to roll down. Her eyes focused in on the belt and holster that the officer carried, so focused that her ears had apparently stopped working. For as long as she could remember she always had a thing for the power of people who carried guns. Quickly reminiscing about a fling she had with street cat, who would always go to bed with his gun on the night stand, and how excited she would get watching him load and unload the clip. The officer spoke again.

"License and registration ma'am!"

Even with the soft speech Veronica could still hear the authority in the officer's voice. Thinking to herself damn, undoing those first three buttons on her blouse was such a waste. Her breasts were just about out, and her Victoria Secrets water bra didn't help matters in the least. She looked up at the officer and smiled as she handed over her identification. Then in an unassuming voice she uttered "Is there a problem officer?"

"Well ma'am besides the fact that you were doing ten over the spend limit, I also noticed you swerving a bit a ways back."

"Really? I wasn't aware that I swerved."

"Yes, ma'am you did! By any chance have you had anything to drink today?"

"I cannot tell a lie officer, yes I have. I had two glasses of wine, but that was all."

"Okay ma'am. Wait here while I go over your information."

Veronica not expecting too much from this infraction, with the exception of a ticket, After all she wouldn't be able to flirt her way out of this predicament as she had done so many times in the past. She could only hope that there would be no points involved. As the officer turned and walked back to the squad car Veronica was able to take advantage of the view, and an enjoyable view it was. The officer stood around 5'4 and was built on the thicker side, though Veronica could tell it wasn't the flabby thickness that she had grown accustomed to. She was toned from the view her uniform showed off. Noticing the beautiful thick hips and thighs Veronica was in awe when she saw how the waist just sunk in. It was the type of body that demanded long shopping trips at the right boutiques to insure getting the proper fit. The officer disappeared into the squad car to review the information, this didn't worry Veronica one bit because she knew her driving record was immaculate after all she had gone to great lengths on several occasions to keep it that way. She didn't dub herself the queen of escaping tickets for no reason. She had serviced more police weapons than any gun shop in Michigan. It was almost as if she sped up anytime a cop was around just to relieve them of their stress.

The officer called the plate and license number in and waited for her report to come back. Only to hear the excitement on the other end of the car's radio.

"So I see you've pulled her over I wish I could trade places with you right now!"

Said a fellow officer on the other end of the radio following up his statement with another, "I sure could use the stress relief right about now." Then he chuckled a few times, and got off the radio. The female officer looked over the computer screen to find absolutely nothing. Veronica's record was clean as a whistle not so much as a parking ticket ever! That was unbelievable, until the officer remembered how a couple of the guys at the station would always kid around about pulling over "The Big Ticket" a wild chick who tends give favorable and pleasurable personal gifts to keep from getting tickets. On top of that about four different cops tried their best to get her patrol route for the night but she wasn't in the mood to switch. Maybe the rumors were true, and she had pulled over "The Big Ticket!" there was only one way to find out.

Walking back to the car the officer had made up her mind and wanted to know for herself just how far Veronica would go to escape a ticket. Better yet how far she would go to repay the kindness of the officer for letting her off with a warning. The window was down as she approached the car, smiling the whole time.

"Well Mrs. Patton I see that you have an immaculate driving record. It would be a shame to ruin that!"

"I agree! I would be more than grateful if we could keep my record intact."

"Is that right?"

During the entire conversation the officer had her eyes planted on Veronica's cleavage. Noticing the officer's eye fixated on her breast Veronica poked her chest out a bit more. All to the enjoyment of the officer.

"Well it's your lucky day Mrs. Patton, I'm gonna let you off with just a warning."

"Well thank you! There are still some decent people left in the world. You are so right it is my lucky day."

"Well you make sure you're careful from here on out."

"I wish there was something I could do to you."

"Excuse me?"

"I meant I wish there was something I could do for you to repay you for your kindness."

"Really?"

The officer smiled and then ran her tongue across her lips. She stared directly into Veronica's eyes with a certain lust that couldn't be mistaken. Returning the same look Veronica refused to break their stare, it was no way in the world they weren't thinking the exact same thing at the exact same moment. Finally breaking the officer turned to walk back to the squad car, not sure of how to pull off what she wanted to take place. Just as she took her first step away she responded one last time. Once the stare was broken Veronica eyes wondered down to the officer's badge number 30469. Thinking to herself what a combination! "A hoe I would love to 69!"

"I would love for you to do something to me!"

Then she walked away, and before Veronica could get her rebuttal out the officer was in her car and slowly pulling off. Veronica threw her car into drive and jumped right behind the officer and followed her back to the hiding place she had jumped out of before pulling Veronica over in the first place. She pulled up in between the two buildings with Veronica pulling in right behind her. Unable to think of something cleaver to say to the officer Veronica got out of her car and walked up to the back of the squad car just as the officer was getting out. Without saying a word the women met at the back of the car. Wasting no time instantly their lips locked, tasting the deliciousness of one another. Veronica seemed to be the more experienced of the two women taking control of the situation. Pushing officer 30469 into the trunk of the squad car while fumbling with her holster. Unbuckling the belt and then the pants, the officer's thick thighs and firm ass was all that kept her pants in place. The heat she was feeling was evident, as Veronica kneeled and tugged at the pants she could feel the moisture immediately. Finally getting the uniform pants to fall, beneath those beautiful legs Veronica made the officer climb on top of the car. As she pushed the female officer back spreading her legs, able to enjoy the muscular pillars. She dipped her head into the inferno; with quick swipes of her tongue she tasted the sweetness of a woman. Sending shockwaves through both of their bodies. She could feel the officer's legs tense up, from the enjoyment. Mumbling as she enjoyed every drop of her new tasty treat!

"Is this what you wanted me to do to you? Is this what you had in mind?"

With nothing more than a moan as an answer the officer grabbed a hand full of Veronica's hair pushing the back of her head deeper into the depths of her abyss. Depriving Veronica's of any type of air, as she tongued her clit quickly and continuously until she could no longer control herself. Her legs went from a mild tremor to an all out shake as if she was having her own personal earthquake. Then as if a dam had broke she released a wave of her sweet nectar into Veronica's waiting mouth. Loving every last drop of her treat Veronica kept her mouth right where it should've been. Finally removing her mouth just before the officer lost all consciousness from the orgasm that she wasn't expecting on this night. Veronica lifted her head and smiled!

"Was this what you had in mind for repayment?"

Unable to respond the officer just laid there for a second until she recovered from the unbelievable ordeal her body had just been through. Veronica wiped her mouth, and then moved away from the car, and the officer. Explaining that she should really be getting home to her husband considering it was getting late. The officer agreed but insisted on the exchange of phone numbers, so she might get another chance to experience this intoxicating feeling again. Just like that Veronica was up and on her way home, turning for just a second and stating "Thanks for letting me off!" then she was in her car and pulling off. Arriving home shortly after her experience she headed straight for the downstairs bathroom for a quick hoe bath, to wipe away the taste of the officer.

Isaac had been working like a Hebrew slave for the past month seven days a week, week after week. He had been so busy with work, he had become quite neglectful of his beautiful wife. So today, he planned to call it quits early and surprise Veronica for lunch in order to celebrate her finishing the plans for Pastor Coleman's birthday event. He asked his secretary to order from Como's her favorite Italian restaurant, so he could stop and pick it up and head home to enjoy a nice romantic afternoon. Canceling the rest of his meetings for the afternoon, he headed out of the office for the day. On his way to Ferndale, to pick up the blackened Chicken Fettuccini dish that Veronica loved so much. Isaac called the house to insure she was home, and not at the gym. With no answer he figured she may not have made it home just yet. Making it to Como's in just fifteen minutes, his order wasn't ready just yet. He decided to wait on the order, at the bar and enjoy a drink. Downing the first triple shot of Jack Daniel's, and quickly ordering the next two before long Isaac had a light buzz. That was just the way he liked it when he was planning to give his wife the ultimate pleasure. Isaac was already a good lover but he always felt that a little liquor usually put him over the top. Just as he downed the third and finally triple shot he noticed a beautiful silhouette that he knew all too well.

The figure disappeared into the women's restroom, and soon reappeared. Not even three minutes had passed, by this time Isaac had made his way to the bathroom door. As the figure opened the door to return to the restaurant Veronica was startled by her husband.

"Hey baby! What are you doing here?"

As startled as she was she was unable to think clearly. Stuck with a lost for words.

"You must have called Kim and she told you where to find me! Damn! It's hard to find good help these days. I wanted it to be a surprise...Well no matter, we still get to spend the day together."

"YES! Baby she can't keep a secret, but don't be too mad at her. I told her I was right around the corner and it didn't make sense for you to go all the way home. So I would surprise you instead."

Veronica grabbed her husband by the waist and pulled him close slipping her tongue into his mouth. At the same time she winked and waved good bye to the woman in uniform that sat alone at a table by the window. Isaac and Veronica walked out of the restaurant then made their way home in separate cars. Veronica forced to multi-task while following her husband home, and talking on her cell. Attempting to explain to the beautiful woman she left sitting in Como's with a stunned look on her face, exactly why she was leaving the restaurant so abruptly. Her phone explanation must not have been enough because soon there were flashing lights in her review mirror.

"I know this isn't you behind me! My husband is right in front of me!"

"I know! Pull over!"

Walking up on the side of her vehicle and tapping on the window, the officer asked Veronica to roll her window down.

"What are you doing?"

"You thought you were gonna get away that easily? You were supposed to be mine this afternoon! I've been waiting for days now and I want my turn. So if I were you I'd be thinking of something to tell my husband, to get out of going home right now."

"You know I am a married woman! My husband took off today just to surprise me! I had no idea he would be at the restaurant, but hell shit happens! I barely came up with an excuse for me being there in the first place. Now you want me to make something up for me to get out of going home with him? That's crazy!"

"Well you better think fast because he is pulling up right now!"

Isaac pulled up after going around the corner, he had called his wife's cell phone twice to find out if everything was okay. Once she didn't answer he figured he would swing back around to check on her. He couldn't think of a reason she had been pulled over considering they weren't even close to a traffic light and the speed limit was 45mph. He pulled up in front of each car to insure he didn't startle the officer approaching with caution, Isaac hollered out to the officer.

"Is there a problem officer? She is my wife."

"No problem at all sir, your wife was just swerving a bit while driving I just wanted to make sure everything was alright. Please return to your car sir."

"Is my wife okay?"

"Yes sir I need you to return to your car sir."

"Honey? Are you okay?"

Veronica leaned her head out of the window and expressed to her husband that she was fine, she was just having trouble finding her proof of insurance. Isaac paused, and took another step forward before the officer repeated herself. Asking him to return to his vehicle. Grabbing his phone from his hip Isaac called his wife once again. Veronica answered this time and once again expressed the fact that she was fine and that everything was okay. She had been given ample time to come up with a suitable excuse for her husband. The officer said to keep from actually writing her a ticket she would be nice enough to follow her home. That way Veronica wouldn't have to take the proof of insurance to the station, later on in the week.

"See Veronica I told you to leave that in the glove box at all times!"

"Isaac I don't need that right now!"

"But baby you know I."

"Listen Isaac go ahead home and I'll met you there."

Turning his car on, then pulling away from the curb. Veronica immediately turned to the officer and gave a serious scowl.

"So what now? What's your plan?"

"Well to be honest I like your plan. Maybe I should follow you to your house and check your proof of insurance."

"What? Are you crazy? Besides the fact that my husband is home take into consideration that no one has ever been to my damn house and no one ever will!"

"Well your husband is expecting me to be following you home can't disappoint him now can we?"

"You are crazy!"

"The way I see it you can either do it my way or you can take the chance of me showing up another time eager to tell your husband what you were really doing at Como's today."

The thought of having the officer follow her home and possibly even having a bit of fun with her intrigued Veronica. But she couldn't possibly do what she was allowing her mind to think, or could she? With the officer hot on her tail she made her way up the road about two miles pulling up just as Isaac was unlocking the front door. He turned and awaited his wife noticing that the police car was pulling up in front of the house shortly after. Isaac explained that it was extremely nice of the officer to follow her home.

"You should offer her some coffee!"

"Okay baby, but can you go up stairs and grab the insurance out of my black purse?"

"No problem Hun. We have to get rid of her quickly, because I want you!"

"Okay, the sooner you find the insurance, the sooner she leaves."

As her husband hit the stairs the officer walked into the house with a huge smile. Offering her a cup of coffee Veronica escorted the officer to the kitchen area. As soon as they entered the kitchen the officer pushed Veronica to the counter, and spent her around. Grabbing her face and attempting to force a kiss out of her. Veronica put up a fight, but could not match the forcefulness of the officer. As their lips finally touched she was quickly reminded of how luscious the beautiful officer's lips were. She could taste the sweetness of the officer's lips, along with a hint of peach from the lip gloss the officer was wearing. As their bodies pressed against each other Veronica could feel the warm wetness escape her hidden paradise, and stroll down her thighs. She was on fire! Between the fact that the officer was turning her completely on and the fact that her husband was upstairs the heat she produced rivaled that of Hell and may have easily surpassed it. The kiss contained all the passion of their first encounter, added to it though was the longing, and wanting of another encounter to take place. But this was not the time nor the place, and if no one else knew this Veronica did. Pulling away from the officer she whispered

"We have to stop!"

"Do we?"

"My husband will be back down stairs at any moment! We need to stop this now! It wouldn't benefit either of us to be caught in this situation. I promise we can make up for this soon! I want you just as bad as you want me, so this is going to happen just not right now!"

"You're right but if not now then when?"

"What time is your shift over?"

"I will be off by ten!"

"Then I will figure something out just give me a call when you get off. I'll figure something out before then. Okay?"

"That sounds good but you better make it happen!"

Another quick kiss and the officer made her way back to the front door. Just in time as Isaac strolled back down the stairs, with the bad news! He was unable to find the proof of insurance. Fortunately Veronica was able to find the information in the bottom of the purse she was carrying. So the officer was more than satisfied, expressing the fact that she had to get back to work. She exited the door without haste, as the couple stood in the door way. Isaac couldn't help but express how utterly nice the officer was, and insist that the force needed more like her. Still partially excited from the encounter, Veronica just nodded in agreement. Then expressed her hunger for not only the food, but more importantly for him.

Chapter 13: *The Charity Dinner*

The party started off without a hitch three of the four guest speakers had already been up for their respective speeches. Each speaker taking their time to say as many kind words about Pastor Coleman as they felt he deserved. The last person was to be the newest star of Detroit. He had been working for the Detroiter for the past year, and was on his way to being the new face of the paper. The pastor would throw a quote from him into a sermon from time to time, constantly calling him a breath of fresh air. Admittedly so he did seem like the one person in the news who told the important stories even if it did make him a few enemies along the way. He was the surprise guest for this event, even though Pastor Coleman had him trapped over at his table since he had entered the event. Mr. Alexander had made the trip thanks to his aunt and uncle. Asia and Terrance weren't the only successful individuals in their family. His uncle only a couple years his elder, wasn't the only one who had been blessed with good looks either. Upon arrival Mr. Alexander had commanded the attention of just about every woman at the event, husband or not the women hawked him as if this wasn't a church event. He was definitely use to the attention because he acted as if he didn't even notice the women of the church attacking him with their eyes. Staying focused on the man of the hour the entire time as if his next article would be based on Pastor Coleman.

After about thirty minutes of sitting with the pastor Chris got up and made his way to the podium. Quickly introducing himself to the crowd not a woman in the building needed that introduction considering their eyes had been fixated on him for the last 45 minutes. Clearing his throat he began.

"Well for those of you who don't know I am so much more comfortable in front of a computer, than this. Though I do have a flare for words they are usually of the written variety. However when my aunt Asia and uncle Terrance told me that Pastor Coleman was one of my biggest supporters. I could barely contain my excitement, this is an unbelievable opportunity to speak on behalf of one of the cities truly great men. As you all must know Pastor Coleman is a legend in the Detroit area. There aren't many people you can talk to in any area that don't have a standing relationship with Pastor Coleman."

Pausing for just a second to turn and look at Pastor Coleman, Chris was greeted with a slight smile. Turning back to the crowd he continued.

"We are here tonight to celebrate the 55 years of a beautiful life, as well as the 30 plus years of service that he has committed to serving GOD, and this community. As most of you already know Pastor Coleman has worked closely with the City's homeless shelters, as well as food and clothing drives. All the while continuing to be a mainstay at any and every event for the Red Cross. And it's because of him that any and everything dealing with each and every event has been and will continue to be a success. I thank you all for joining me in thanking him for being an inspiration to all of us. HAPPY BIRTHDAY Pastor Coleman!!!"

With that Mr. Alexander led the entire party in wishing the pastor a Happy Birthday in the traditional way. By simply singing him a couple bars of Happy Birthday. Jokingly throwing a Cha, cha, cha in between each chorus. Pastor Coleman ventured up to the podium with a smile that stretched across his entire face. He hadn't felt this honored in years, and hadn't felt this good since Mrs. Coleman was alive. He kept his appreciation speech relatively short considering dinner was on it's way out and he was hell bent on finding out what a hundred dollar plate of food taste like.

During dinner everyone mingled and took the opportunities to meet the Celebs that came out and spoke on the pastor's behalf. More than a fair share of women took the time to introduce themselves to Mr.

Alexander included in that long list was Veronica. She was one of the few that actually got the attention of the journalist; she managed to get the eye contact that the other women had only hoped for. He was almost stunned by her unbelievable beauty; he quickly noticed the more than impressive ring that Veronica wore on the four finger of her left hand. Normally this would've been an instant turn-off for him, but for some reason Chris didn't shut down as quickly this time. Holding their short conversation seconds longer than he knew they should. He couldn't help himself, and even as she made her way back to her table. He was still unable to take his eyes off her as she sashayed away. Veronica was quite aware of the set of eyes following her back to her seat, but what she hadn't noticed was that her mother-in-law's eyes were also working overtime as well. Eye's that she definitely didn't want following her, but unfortunately this was something she had no control of and more importantly could do nothing about.

Mrs. Patton-Silver noticed something was definitely different about Veronica. The woman who had spent countless hours of her life dieting and hitting the gym seemed to be letting her age catch up with her. Everyone takes a certain hit at a certain time in the weight gain department especially us not fortunate enough to have round the clock fitness experts at our disposal. Mrs. Patton-Silver couldn't help but notice that this wasn't the case with Veronica. Her weight gain was slight but to the trained eye was definitely noticeable. She was carrying her extra weight in her checks and not the ones below the waist. Add that to the minuet bulge that the black loose fitting dress that she chose for the occasion was barely showing and you have two parts to the equation with only one part left. That part would be answered later in tonight's festivities, and that only meant one thing. Mrs. Patton-Silver would have her eyes on Veronica and her eating habits for the rest of the night.

There were definite signs if what Mrs. Patton-Silver thought was going on really was going on. She would be able to tell if she was right by only two ways at this point. First, Veronica has never been one to pass up a drink no matter what the circumstances were she would have one if it was offered. Second, she was never a big eater at least not in a public venue. She would always order a salad or something light and even then she would seem to disappear after only a couple bites. No doubt to find the nearest bathroom to get rid of the food she refused to allow to digest. Well that was always her mother-in-laws thought. Either way these would be the tell all signs, and the eagle eyed Mrs. Patton-Silver wouldn't let her out of her sight tonight. As the night continued Mrs. Patton-Silver would have all the proof she needed to confront Isaac with her assumption. She had no choice, Mrs. Patton-Silver would have to tell her son about Veronica once and for all and this time he would have to listen. Waiting until the event was coming to an end and all her information was gathered Mrs. Patton-Silver insisted that Isaac escort her to the limousine that she had waiting.

"Isaac, I need you to understand that I am telling you this for your own good. I've told you time and time again, but you never listen. Isaac, I'm tired of saving you from yourself."

"Again mother? What is it this time?"

"Shhh…Shut your mouth and listen! That hussy that you call a wife is no good…She doesn't deserve you and she definitely doesn't deserve to be in this family! She is nothing more than a trashy whore! It's about time you wake up and realize the truth I know it, Hell…half of the Metro Detroit area knows it."

"Dammitt!!! I can't believe you are starting this again…Veronica is my wife, and I love her. I've told you before there isn't anything you can do about that."

"Isaac…You never did have much common sense…Especially when dealing with women every time a woman gives you a little attention or let you smell her stankin ass, you fall for whatever she offers…This tramp has your nose so open that you can't even see that she's making a fool of you."

"What mother? What is it this time? What are you blaming on Veronica this time?"

"Isaac, you are a fool…you won't be satisfied until that gold digger takes you for everything you have. She has you blinded, but not me…She might have you fooled but she will never have me! Wake up and inhale deeply, take in a good whiff of that shit she's serving because I promise you that isn't the smell of roses. Maybe this will finally wake you up. Did you notice tonight that she didn't take one drink? Better yet did you notice her unbelievable eating habits? At no point did she get up and run to the bathroom as she is so prone to do."

"So what mother! What are you saying? What's your point?"

"What I'm saying is simple Isaac! Have you not noticed that extra bulge in her stomach area? That whore you married is pregnant!"

"What? That's impossible! Mother I'm tired of you disrespecting my wife! I have existed in your world too long and it is finally time for me to live my life! That means I will no longer listen to you put my wife down, nor will I listen to you disrespect our marriage."

Without so much as another word Isaac retreated from the car, his face filled with anger and mind racing at the unbelievable accusation that his mother offered. Isaac was no fool, and he was tired of being considered on by his mother. Mrs. Patton-Silver was never one to respect his decision about Veronica, and ever since she found out about the choice she was hell bent on correcting the mistake she felt he had made. As hard as she tried, Mrs. Patton-Silver had never gone this far before. But this couldn't be possible, or could it?

Chapter 14: The Visit

After another unbelievable conversation with his mother, filled with accusations and disturbing news Isaac's mind was overrun with questions. "Could his mother have been right all this time? Had he truly been fooled by the woman who truly had his heart? She was his wife, she couldn't possibly do this to him." All these things and more ran through his mind from the time he picked up the phone until the time he actually got to his doctor's office for his unplanned visit. As he walked into the office he was immediately greeted by the nursing staff. One of the long term nurses who was more than on top of the schedule, asked with a certain concern in her voice if everything was okay. Referring to Isaac by his last name, to which he just smile and nodded. Thinking to himself, if he knew everything was okay he wouldn't be sitting in the doctor's office right now. But there was no need to chew her head off about the situation. She was just doing her job and pretending to be concerned.

Nearly an hour had passed and he was still sitting in the lobby, on just about every visit he wondered why he kept this particular doctor. He never keeps times, or appointments and every time Isaac had ever visited the offices it always turned out to be an extremely long visit. Just as his patience was wearing thin a gentleman a little more than three times his age walked out of the back of the office. Smiling and looking like he was in the best shape of his life. As he walked past he politely spoke to Isaac and gave him just a bit of advice.

"Make sure you take care of yourself while you're young it'll be well worth it in the future."

Isaac smiled and rose up out of his seat being summoned by the nurses to the back. As he walked to the back the nurse let him know that the doctor would be right with him. Showing him to one of the six rooms in the back.

"Mr. Patton Dr. Philmoore didn't give us much information for your exam today, but he wants you to get undressed."

Again with nothing more than a nod he allowed the nurse to exit the room. Starting to undress as the door closed, Isaac still couldn't believe the reason he was there. He still wanted so badly to hold on to the trust and love that his relationship was built on. He loved his wife, and he couldn't believe that she could do what she was accused of. His mother had to be wrong, and if she wasn't there was some other explanation for the condition. Dr. Philmoore walked into the room, with a serious look stretched across his face.

"Isaac I got your message this morning and I pulled your last check up charts. They showed that everything was in order, and nothing had changed from any of you past charts."

"Well Doc I still want to retake the test!"

"I understand that I can do the test and get the test results immediately myself."

"I would appreciate that."

"For you Isaac anything if it wasn't for your mother and her help I probably wouldn't have these offices today."

"I do appreciate you keeping the reason for my visit undisclosed. I want to be the first and the only person to know about these results today."

"That's not a problem Isaac, but I have to ask is everything alright?"

"Honestly I can't answer that until I get these test results back. But everything will be fine either way."

"Well in that case I'm going to need a sample and I also need to run a couple of tests the entire process shouldn't take more than an hour or two. Does that work for you?"

"That will be fine Doc."

Isaac sat there thinking the entire time as he took the test that Dr. Philmoore needed to give him the news that he so desperately needed.

Seconds passed like minutes, and minutes, like hours an hour seemed like an eternity. Isaac grew restless, and impatient he wanted, no he needed answers and they just weren't coming quick enough. As he sat on the table awaiting his results a million questions ran through his mind. The time frame that Dr. Philmoore threw out was so far from accurate that Isaac decided to get up and find out what was taking so long. Just as he was getting ready to open the door to the room Dr. Philmoore was turning the knob to come through.

"Well I have some news, but it's no different than any other visit. The tests came back negative, so everything is still the same."

With every ounce of hope snatched away, Isaac's only hope was that his wife had nothing new to inform him of. But the observations of his mother were running through his head at a mile a minute. His attempts at holding back his anger weren't going well. All that was left to do was thank Dr. Philmoore for his time and go home and have a discussion with his wife. With a quick glance at his watch, he noticed that he only had a short period of time before Veronica was scheduled to leave for a meeting. He had no choice, but to get home quick.

October was back again which meant Homecoming season was here. When speaking of Homecoming no one did it better than Morris Brown College. Well at least that's what the alum's of the prestigious college believed and you couldn't tell them otherwise. It was an event for all ages. The students of the present, the recent graduates, and of course the alumni of old. They all would come together and enjoy some school spirit. There was no bigger supporter than Terrance and Asia having graduated from Morris Brown almost ten years ago they hadn't missed a Homecoming event since, and were two of the biggest supporters. Every year around the same time they would drop everything and hop a flight down to Atlanta GA and party like there was no tomorrow. The usually reserved Terrance lost all inhibitions once he stepped off the plane. To be totally honest it was one of the few times that Asia actually enjoyed her husband. She wished that she got this side of him all the time, but knowing that her wish was impossible she accepted what she could get.

Events had been planned from the beginning of the week all the way pass the actual Home Coming night. Considering they were already late by Terrance's mental clock there would be no rest for the next four days. It was Thursday and Terrance felt that they should've actually got there on Monday for the pre-parties. The parties were nonstop and so was Terrance, no sooner than they were off the plane the rush began. There was a rush to get to the bags, then a rush to get to the rental car, followed by a rush to get to the hotel. It was nonstop, and Terrance wouldn't have it any other way. The entire time Terrance was on the phone attempting to find out where everyone would be tonight. There was only one person to call for that information, Mr. Homecoming himself, TJ was the epitome of Morris Brown Alumni. He not only stayed on after graduation to help recruit new students, but he also started the alumni committee. He more importantly was one of the people responsible for keeping the learning doors open, considering all the added revenue he help bring in with his vast connections. When TJ sponsored a party or hell even said he would be in the building that's where the masses flocked to.

Tonight's party was scheduled to be at Sugar Hill, and everyone was supposed to be there. Sugar Hill wasn't one of those upscale uppity events people that visit Atlanta had become accustomed to. Sugar Hill located in Underground was for that group of people from other states who wanted a feel of home. Being from Detroit, this was about as close as your were gonna get without fighting your way out at the end of the night. It was a two level event, from the second level you could look over the balcony and see the dance floor. This wasn't the place for tonight's party at least not from Terrance's opinion; he was ready to get loose and party. He headed straight for the lower level, where he was sure the party was going to be. It was already 11:00 and he knew that most of his people were already there. He couldn't have been more right; as he and Asia walked through the curtains they turned to the left noticing most of the crowd was MB alumni. Terrance wasted no time greeting everyone with a huge smile and excited yell. Cupping his hands around his mouth for the bull horn effect, Terrance grabbed everyone's attention with the longest one word greeting that excited everyone in the immediate area.

"HOOOOOOOOOOMMMMMMMMMMMMMMEEECOMMMM MMMMMMMMMIIIIINNNNNNNNNNNNNNNNNNNNGG"

Just about everyone one in the area turned with smiles and you even heard it echoed back throughout the club. It was the universal Morris Brown homecoming chant. Terrance started the ripple affect someone else hit it just as he finished, and then another person screamed it as well. It kept going for about ten minutes. By then Terrance and Asia were greeting everyone personally, ordering drinks and laughing and joking. Exchanging pleasantries with hugs going round the room. Just as quick as the drinks were ordered Terrance downed them and ordered more. He was hell bent on catching up with the rest of the place.

Asia quietly mingled through the crowd, flashing her pearly whites and waving to the distant friends. She floated through the room with a certain air, her outfit clinging to all the right curves. The diet and exercise regiment that she refused to slack up on had paid off. As confident as Asia portrayed herself to be she was still obsessed with how everyone else viewed her. She had to be the hottest and trendiest at all times. There is nothing wrong with not wanting to be caught on a bad day but Asia took that thought process to another level. Especially once she got around her Sorors! The one thing that separated her from other typical mirror carriers was she was a bit more approachable. Add to that she was already purposed and driven before she joined she was an assets to the organization not the other way around. Even though Asia only attended Morris Brown for one year before she transferred to Spelman, she made her mark on the school making some friends for life.

The party was going crazy and just when you thought it wouldn't get any wilder in walked TJ. Always late to everything TJ viewed it more as being fashionably late, but considering two hours had passed and he was just entering the building at 1:00 a.m. There was nothing fashionable about his tardiness. TJ started the party off the same way Terrance had done earlier in the night. With a loud and long yell of "homecoming" in a way that only a true MBC alum could. By this time Terrance was so excited that he grabbed one of the high stools from one of the tables. Climbing up and standing on it, cupping his hands together one more time and let it rip once again. By this time he was on his sixth drink and still ordering more. TJ did what he did best immediately heading for the dance floor as if he was back in Detroit. He was known as the Hustle, and Stepping king in these parts. If there was a new dance TJ not only knew how to do it, but he regularly would add his own spin to it and make it his. The party went on for the next two hours before they started shutting the club down for the night. It was just in time too because Terrance didn't need anything else to drink.

Asia got Terrance into the rental and drove to the hotel, they decided to stay downtown so they wouldn't have far to commute for all the events on the weekend. There was only one extra drive that would be made on this visit to Atlanta. Terrance had been talking shit for the last two homecoming trips and Asia was finally going to pull his card and shut him the hell up! They wouldn't be partying tomorrow night with their old school chums, no Asia had other plans for there night.

Waking up the next morning with a horrible taste in his mouth, Terrance's head was pounding. He got up and struggled to the bathroom in search of some type of relief. Asia had prepared the bathroom just the way he liked it, knowing that from past experience he would need his aspirin and a room temperature bottled water. Cracking the seal on the aspirin, and twisting open the water it took one gulp to get rid of the pills and two more before the 16 ounce bottle was empty. Terrance turned on the shower, full blast of nothing but hot water and shut the bathroom door. It didn't take long for the small bathroom to fill with steam, as Terrance took care of the first part of the three S's in preparation of completing the second part shortly there after. As he sat there and the heat from the shower allowed the perspiration to poor from his forehead he could feel the aspirin taking affect almost immediately. Finishing his business, and jumping in the shower it was less than thirty minutes and Terrance was now prepared for today's agenda.

He exited the bathroom with nothing more than a plush robe provided by the luxury suite. He couldn't help but notice that his wife still laid there enjoying her slumber. He could see the curves of her magnificent body covered by nothing but the thin sheet that she laid under. Terrance could see a hint of blue but that was as much the sheet allowed, he wanted to see just what he missed out on last night after making it to the hotel. Moving closer to the bed as quietly as possible he slowly removed the sheet, and really enjoyed the view. He was speechless; his wife's body was immaculate. She was so toned and defined from her calves, to her upper thigh. The muscle wasn't that of a bodybuilder but more of an Olympic track star. As his eyes traveled further up he enjoyed the flatness of her firm abs, which led him to her beautiful breast. To be honest those were the very first thing that he noticed when he first met his wife, but he only admitted to being mesmerized by her eyes. He could feel himself growing by the second, by just looking at his wife. Thinking that this would be a great way to start off the morning he leaned in and gently kissed his wife on her cheek, at the same time running his hand from the back of her knee straight up her thigh. Asia slightly moaned as her husband gently touched her. The excitement was mounting quickly for Terrance, as he kissed his wife deeply she could feel all the thickness that he had to offer. In her mind she was hoping, but all her lower regions new better. She was in for a quick session and him getting a quick explosion, leaving her to satisfy herself. In her mind they were already midway through the act, as unfortunate as this was it was also the truth. Terrance barely got himself through three strokes and his body was already trembling. Ready for the explosion that surely should have come at least thirteen minutes from now for him to even be considered a decent lover. Asia regularly tried to convince herself that it was just her, and her oasis was just that good. Though having the tightest and wettest, somehow never seemed to comfort her on those nights when she had to finish the job herself. Rolling over to the other side of the bed Terrance was breathing hard from his orgasm while his wife laid there pissed and unsatisfied. Thinking to herself that he couldn't possibly think that she was happy with this as a matter of fact she was wondering how long she had been unsatisfied.

There wasn't much getting done today; Terrance was knocked out from he and his wife's workout from earlier in the day. Finally waking up for the second time he rolled over to find his wife wasn't next to him. Immediately he jumped up to look for his wife, with renewed energy he was ready for whatever tonight. That was a good thing too because what Asia had in store was going to take all the energy he had. As he entered the living room of the suite he noticed his wife sitting on the couch on her cell. As Terrance went to speak she threw her finger up to her lips telling him without words to be quiet. Not too much time went by and she was off the phone and telling him it was time to get dressed. They had reservations for the night, and she didn't want to be late.

It took Terrance about forty five minutes to get dressed as his wife waited for him with a smile on her face. For some reason or another she was extremely excited about tonight's adventure. Asia had plans, and even though Terrance was in the dark he still had a good feeling about tonight. As they got off the elevator Asia started towards the front door instead of moving towards the door that led to the garage.

"Asia you know we parked in the garage."

"Yes, but we aren't driving."

"Oh who we riding with? Is TJ picking us up?"

"No Hun, not tonight! Actually I'm hoping we don't run into any MBC people tonight."

With a devilish smirk she, continued to walk out of the revolving doors with her husband a half a step behind her. As they stepped out into the chilled Atlanta night air, they stood in front of an all black limo with the windows heavily tinted. The driver stood by the back passenger side door awaiting their arrival. With the door already open Asia walked directly to the car and stepped in. Terrance stood there for a second attempting to figure out just where it was they were going tonight. His wife looked stunning but she wasn't overly dressed and she allowed him to just throw on some slacks and a blazer instead of a suit. So it couldn't be that serious, but she went as far as to rent a limo. That was enough to have him baffled as to where they were going to end up tonight. Finally jumping into the back seat with his wife he looked at her with a confused stare. To which she responded without even looking his way.

"We'll be there soon so stop worrying so much! Besides I really think you are going to have fun tonight. I know I am!"

Terrance sat back in his seat and just enjoyed the soft music that was playing. There were many differences between Detroit and Atlanta the biggest one being how spread out Atlanta was in comparison to Detroit, if there was one thing you could do without in Atlanta it was definitely the traffic. So the statement that Asia made saying they were going to be there shortly was in fact sadly mistaken. It seemed as if an hour had passed before they were finally pulling up to their destination. The driver pulled up directly to the door, considering the way the front door was lit up you would think they had just pulled up to the MGM grand in Detroit. Terrance knew better than that, but still wasn't sure were he was considering he didn't get a look at the moniker on the building as they were pulling in. As they removed themselves from the car, and entered the building Terrance noticed that the crowd was dressed with the intent to impress, he thought to himself and then whispered to his wife.

"Maybe we are a bit under dressed."

"It doesn't matter Terrance or at least it won't."

Still surveying the room for Terrance was intrigued to know exactly were they were. At the same time he was impressed by the atmosphere. As they walked through to the first set of doors and down the hall Terrance noticed that the restaurant/slash club for some reason had changing rooms. Asia kept walking right pass them, but they definitely caught Terrance's eye. Where the hell were they was all Terrance could think to himself. The club's music wasn't as loud as it could've been, but the club was huge with a huge wood floor that stretched across the room. It also had a couple chairs and tables set up throughout but the main focus was the dance floor. The bar was at the far end of the club, and was pretty packed it seemed as if everyone was starting their night at the bar. With a couple of people dancing wildly on the floor the couple made there way through the party. Terrance had a hard time controlling his eyes as he walked through the women were beautiful; of course none could hold a candle to his wife. But there were a couple that were truly giving her a run for her money.

The dance floor had two brass poles in the middle a good distance apart. One of the women had a skimpy black dress on that barely came below her butt and seemed to be inching up. She had a pair of heels on that screamed out pain for her feet, they had to be at least six to eight inches. Terrance couldn't tell, at just a glance and had already felt he had his eye on her too long as it was. His wife grabbed his hand and pulled him with her to the next room. This room was totally different, still beautiful in it's on right it was more intimate and would be their destination for dinner. With a smile on his face as they finally arrived at their table Terrance spoke to his wife.

"Asia where are we?"

"What's wrong Terrance you uncomfortable? Or you just don't like it?"

"Uncomfortable? Why would I be uncomfortable? It's just a club. Actually it's really nice, I like it."

"Good I'm glad you like it. We are gonna have a good time tonight.

As his wife ended her sentence, Terrance broke eye contact with her and noticed a beautiful full figured dark woman sitting with a gentleman a couple tables away. All he could make out in the dimness was her eyes and that was because they were fixated on him. If they weren't she was definitely looking at something directly behind him. Terrance quickly turned away not wanting to give the woman the wrong idea. He didn't want to upset Asia either they were having a great night and he didn't need wandering eyes to ruin the moment. Asia and Terrance talked for the next twenty minutes before the waitress showed up with their drinks. To Terrance's surprise the waitress place his glass in front of him without a word and one whiff told the secret of the glass. It was his favorite drink, Hennessey mixed with Bailey's. Terrance was shocked he didn't even order anything and they bought him his favorite. The waitress placed a glass of wine in front of Asia, once again he was confused. Without a word Asia took a sip of her wine and smiled, then excused herself to the ladies room. She also wanted to get a look at the rest of the establishment. As she left the table she entered the next room and suddenly realized that if they wanted to start dinner they would have to get up and serve themselves. The gourmet buffet area had her mouth watering; this wasn't your usual buffet. The food looked as if it was prepared by Emeril himself easily rivaling any of the best restaurants. After a quick glance at the food she moved to the ladies room a bit faster. Upon entering she noticed that the ladies room was just as plush as the rest of the club. It wasn't just a rest room but also a spa area for the ladies. She caught a small shock when she turned the corner and ran into a group of women more than enjoying themselves in the walk in shower area. Asia was more aroused than shocked, but still seemed startled. She tried to turn and walk away but her legs were locked, and so were her eyes on the group of women.

Terrance was sitting there still a bit confused but the more he surveyed the room the more it started to come to him. Though he was still not completely clear he had noticed the room was full of couples mingling with couples or at least a third party. He also noticed that the beautiful woman had not stopped looking at him yet. Not only was she staring but she had took, Asia's departure as a sign that it was okay for her to stop by their table. Terrance wasn't unfamiliar with attracting women but none had ever been so bold as to approach while he was actually with his wife. The chocolate woman with shoulder length jet black hair stood next to the table, looking down at Terrance she was far from petite. Though she carried her weight well and with such confidence the size 18 that Terrance had easily eyeballed and guessed could have easily been a 22. She had an absolutely gorgeous smile with beautiful full lips, that literally screamed kiss me over and over again. Terrance explained that he was here with his wife Asia and she wouldn't appreciate the company. The woman smiled even harder and responded softly.

"Well maybe I should go and get permission."

She walked away from the table and headed towards the ladies restroom. Walking with the determination of a woman on a mission, she planned to find Asia. Still stuck in the same spot enjoying the view of the women enjoying the taste of one another Asia, felt her own moisture beginning to drip. Just as she turned to head for her own personal stall, she nearly knocked down the beautiful woman who was in search of her. She was so close that as soon as Asia turned the two women nearly locked lips.

"Oh I am sorry, I didn't see you there!"

"Don't worry I saw you. Actually I was looking for you. I noticed you at the table with your husband, you guys make a beautiful couple."

"Well th...thank you."

"No need to be so shy we are all comfortable here. By the way my name is Layla"

Asia noticed the same thing that her husband noticed when first looking at Layla her lips had an uncanny ability to draw you in, and make your mind think dirty thoughts. Asia was mesmerized, by the lips, and the thoughts of what she might be able to do with them. Between that and the fact that her juices were beginning to flow down her inner thigh she would've agreed to just about anything. She just wanted to get to the stall, so she could clean the mess her eyes had allowed her to make.

Asia and her knew chocolate friend returned from the ladies room better acquainted than when each of them left, returning to Terrance who had also made himself comfortable by finding his way to the buffet area and making himself a plate. With a light plate Terrance just wanted to line his stomach to help deal with the night of drinking he had in front of him. Surprised at the fact that his wife was with the beautiful woman, that had just left the table Terrance looked up from his plate and smiled.

"So I see she found you honey."

With a slightly dazed look on her face, mainly because she was still attempting to recover from the scene she had just viewed in the ladies room Asia responded: "So she has!" Layla assumed she had her work cut out for her with the seemingly inexperienced couple. She interrupted them with a sly smile, and then asked the question that had been running through both their minds.

"So what did you guys have in mind for tonight?"

Both pausing and looking at each other before turning their attention back to Layla. They both stuttered along as if they weren't sure how to answer the question. Luckily for them as quickly as Layla had posed the question she took the time retract it. Following up with the Vegas theme;

"What happens at the Trapeze stays at the Trapeze!"

With a beautiful smile Layla insisted that she give the couple the grand tour of the facilities. Terrance and Asia followed Layla through each room more excited from one room to the next. The further they journeyed, they began to notice the less people tend to be wearing. The bar area was illuminated with a bluish fluorescent light, and packed with people draped over each other. Some engulfed in conversation, while others taking full advantage of their surroundings. Asia and Terrance were busy in their own right becoming Voyeurs. Another drink downed, and the couple became a bit less timid. Instead of shying away or blushing Asia and Terrance were now allowing themselves to enjoying everything their eyes had the pleasure of viewing.

Escaping the lure of the bar area Layla then led them to the next area, with a more intimate setting. The room kept the theme of dim lights in, but took comfort to the next level. Instead of tables and chairs the entire area had nothing but sectionals. The couches could almost be considered beds, with more than enough room to enjoy yourself at great lengths. With one more glass of wine any inhibitions that Asia may have been feeling before had totally disappeared. As she became more and more playful with her husband. Not bothered in the least by Layla being on the couch with them. She turned her husbands head to her and looked at him deeply. Terrance's tolerance was a bit higher than that of his wife, so unfortunately for her he wasn't quite in the same place his wife was. Though this wasn't one of those times that she was going to accept him ignoring her pass. She ran her hand across his thigh in search of the member that rarely satisfied her craving. To her surprise Terrance was feeling the mood! Layla sat there enjoying the view of the married couple starting a game that she knew she would've loved to become a part of. The women sitting on either side of Terrance, Asia turned his head towards Layla as she ran her lips and tongue across his neck. Her hands running down the front of his Button-Up releasing his perfectly chiseled chest, which was still confined to a white undershirt. Slowly pressing down on the shirt and releasing the imprint of the abs that Terrance's two a day workouts blessed him with. Layla eyes bulged, she knew he was in shape from the way his clothes hugged his frame but she had no idea how good a choice she had made. She followed Asia's hand as it traveled down to her husband's pants, ready to unleash all Terrance had to offer.

Mentally stuck Terrance had no idea what to do should he; indulge in the event or should he show restraint. He was in a position that just about every man on the planet had dreamed of, but this wasn't just some random act. This was his wife, and he had to be sure this was what she wanted. If it wasn't and she was just attempting to please him or even worse if she was just intoxicated. What would the repercussions be? Luckily his mental stress didn't need much swaying. Layla leaned in and inhaled the aroma of Terrance, as Asia placed kisses on his chest while on her journey lower. No sooner than Layla leaned in Asia reached out and grabbed the back of her hair and clinched tight pulling Layla forward. Her full luscious lips, with a light gloss to them didn't almost do anything this time. And there was no mistake to it. As Asia pressed her lips to Layla's lips, both women slightly open their mouths and tilted their heads. The heat from the women, along with the visual affect, took Terrance to a new height! The pressure in his pants burst out and did the rest of the work for Asia, as his fully erect member escaped from its imprisonment. Terrance had ACTION, and he was ready to perform his duties. The vision was enough in itself, Terrance watched as the two women kissed and fondled each other right over him. Unconcerned at the time that his eyes weren't the only ones watching, as a matter of fact, the room filled with willing watchers of the event.

With the best seat in the house Terrance gazed at his wife with their beautiful new friend. Taking the time to enjoy each woman's body, as he raced his hands across the full figures of both women. They were in their own world by now, thanks mainly to Terrance. Each woman had their skirts hiked up allowing him to explore them with his fingers and hands. As Asia and Layla allowed their tongues to wrestle within their mouths with each flicker of their tongues the enjoyment of the moment became more intense. Terrance had no trouble gauging from the steady flow of their juices onto his waiting finger tips. Deciding to no longer be just the third party Terrance decided to introduce a new taste to the ladies party. Sliding two fingers deep inside his wife, and quickly pulling them out, then placing his fingers between the lips of the two ladies. Asia's taste was exquisite and sent both women into overdrive. Ripping the rest of their clothes off, and to the floor Layla pushed past Terrance and placed Asia gently on her back. Spreading her legs wide allowing the pure beauty of her lower lips to be exposed. Layla laid her lower half over Terrance lap, in perfect position for a spanking. She reached over and enjoyed a spread that couldn't be matched by the buffet line, and Layla planned to have her fill of this meal. The voluptuous thighs and thick dark chocolate cheeks that lay on his lap screamed to be groped. The aroma of vanilla filled his nostrils Victoria Secrets had done its job on this night! Terrance couldn't take being left out anymore, reaching behind him on a table filled with condoms pulling the first three wrappers down he hadn't hit the jack pot yet. Until he reached the fourth time and found what his heart desired. The black wrapper was larger than the rest, and was the only thing that fit him comfortably. Ripping it open and pulling out his protection for the night, Terrance grabbed himself and began the process of getting all of himself into the only thing tighter than what he was planning to get into. Sliding from beneath Layla and positioning himself directly behind her. Then looking to his wife for the okay, to which he couldn't actually receive because she was mentally at a totally different location. The trickiest of tongues hand nothing on Layla, and she was working complete magic on Asia at this moment. Nothing could break the trance they were in, nothing except feeling the thickness of Terrance penetrating her passion from behind. With a perfect arch formed as she accepted all that Terrance had to offer. With nothing more than a light gasp as he gave her every inch of himself the trance was broken for a short while.

Asia was shocked by her husband's act, but at the same time she was turned on. Watching the expression on Terrance' face, as he worked the beautiful woman in front of him. As Layla got use to the stroke and depth of her companion she steadied herself to the rhythmic motion. Putting her Kegel exercises to good use, tightening her muscles as he entered, and loosening them as he retreated. She was a pro, when it came to getting all she wanted out of sex, and right now what she wanted was for this moment to last. After she got the lower half in order she went right back into pleasing Asia so she had no reason to feel left out. It was just in time because Asia's mind had began to wonder a bit passed the encounter. Thinking to herself "He is about to cum any second now." but that thought was immediately erased as Layla cupped her lips around Asia's clit. Creating suction and instantly pushing Asia to climatic heights she had never experienced before. Her legs began to vibrate uncontrollably as she grabbed the back of Layla's head to insure she didn't move an inch. The excitement of Asia's aggressiveness gave way to Layla as she released the suction and lowered her lips a bit to enjoy the fruits of her hard work. As Asia released her flood gates, a river of her essence strolled over Layla's lips and tongue sending shockwaves through Layla's body. Almost immediately her lower muscles reversed the motions. Allowing Terrance unlimited access, but clinching tight as he tried to retreat. That was all it took for Terrance! About three good strokes and it was over erupting while still inside his host. Layla could feel the condom filling up with his warm love juice. The excitement of satisfying the couple was enough to push Layla over the edge as she felt herself release turning her already warm love box, into a hot and steamy sauna!

The three individuals laid there in a state of shock, at the excitement they had just produced. Heavy breathing and grunts and moans were all they could muster. Layla, knew the night had just began and was hoping for a round two. The same thought was on Asia's mind, now she only hoped she could get Terrance to join as she looked down to the other end of the couch he was already up and prepared for round two and the enjoyment of his wife. Their night didn't end until the following morning, awaking fully hung over with a third party nestled in the bed between them.

Their unbelievable night was easily the highlight of this vacation. There wasn't anything that could possibly surpass the night of passion they had both just experience. Using the same remedy that Terrance enjoyed the day before to relieve their headaches. Getting rid of their headaches was essential considering today was the parade, and everyone who is anyone would be there. Layla awoke and wasted no time grabbing her garments and heading straight for the bathroom. The couple just starred at each other as they continued to lay in the bed. After, ten minutes Layla returned from the bathroom fully dressed. Addressing the couple as she stood there as stunning as she was the night before.

"Well I had a wonderful time with you guys last night. I truly hope that the feeling is mutual."

The couple stammered and stumbled over their words as they attempted to get out their agreement on the beautiful time spent of the prior night. Not wanting them to feel anymore uncomfortable, Layla placed her business card on the table as she exited the bedroom of the suite heading for the door. Before they could get themselves together they heard the door close behind them and just like that Layla was gone.

With nothing left to do for the day except hit the parade and enjoy everyone being on the yard. Asia and Terrance took their time getting ready, neither one of them daring to speak on the previous night's encounters. It was a quiet morning, up until they finally arrived on campus. Missing the parade because in the recent years their historically black college was merely a shell of its former glory. Mainly because of mismanagement, add that to the pride and the fear of the bishops who were in charge. Enrollment was down drastically, and their accreditation had been pulled at least two years prior. The only thing that did keep it afloat was alumni support, and the generosity of the professors who would lend their time, and credentials pro bono. It was finally beginning to show during the homecoming festivities, the usually unattainable yard of the campus had be overrun with venders this year. Selling everything from clothes and jewelry, to books and cds. Any other year you would find these same vendors, on your way to the campus or even down the street from the campus. But to bring in more revenue the college allowed them access to the yard for a small donation undoubtedly.

The fraternities and sororities still had their plots and respective areas maintained. To the new students, and any passer-by who didn't know any better the event would have definitely looked normal. Maybe to a person new to the area, it may have looked massive but to the MBC faithful there was a difference. If you couldn't tell by the numbers, then it would've been the whispers that could be heard just by walking past certain groups. Everyone was happy to be here, but there was definitely a difference. The partying and stepping went on and everyone still found a way to enjoy themselves. Catching up with old college friends, some of whom hadn't been seen in years and some who hadn't been seen since last year. Asia and Terrance were embraced by them all with love, and before they knew it time had flown by the day had merged with the night and they had a flight to catch tomorrow.

Chapter 15: *Confrontations*

After an unbelievable trip to the doctor Isaac realized the undeniable truth. His mother was right all along. She was the only woman he could trust. Because the woman he had fallen head over heels in love with was a liar and an adulteress. If she had the gall to lie about something like this, Lord only knew what else she was capable of. His mother tried time and time again to warn him of the possibilities that he may face dealing with Veronica, but as a stubborn child usually does he had to learn this on his own and he did learn, the hard way! Now with the proof he would have the unpleasant job of confronting the love of his life and her lies. Driving home dazed and confused the speedometer told the tale of how heavy this burden was. He was in no hurry to have this head on collision with Veronica. Because as honest as he had been throughout their marriage he too had a secret.

Arriving at the house just in time to catch Veronica, before she got in the car for her meeting at the church. Isaac pulled up in the drive way directly behind her and got out almost before the car had stopped. Surprised by his actions Veronica immediately asked was everything okay. Isaac explained that everything was fine and followed it with the statement.

"We need to talk!"

With sternness in his voice that Veronica had rarely heard from him. Immediately she became worried, but didn't let on that she was through action. Wondering what the problems was she let everything race through her mind at once. Hoping it was something simple like work or his mother once again she stopped and followed him back into the house. For a split second she thought that maybe her indiscretions may have come back to haunt her, but she easily ruled that out because he seemed a bit too calm. Even though she had never seen Isaac even seem as if he could lose his cool demeanor she knew that even he would have to blow up if all her dirt was ever to surface. Heading straight for the living room and asking Veronica to have a seat Isaac definitely had something on his mind.

"Babe I have something I need to tell you but first, I have a question."

"Okay Isaac ask me."

"Veronica are you pregnant?"

"What made you ask me that? I just took the test yesterday. It was positive but it might not be right...I wasn't going to bring it to your attention until I had gone to the doctor to be sure. This may just be some mistaken home test that we are talking about here. This pregnancy isn't fact!

Dropping his head in disappointment Isaac exhaled and let out a deep sigh. Furious on the inside but showing wonderment with his body language. Isaac was torn apart about his wife, and her decisions.

"Don't tell me your mother has been talking to you again? Is that what this is about the great Mrs. Patton-Silver is on another war path and can't stand to see her precious son ruin his life with the wicked wife he choose! She can't stand to see her fairy tale life take a turn that she didn't carefully calculate while planning out your future! Is this what we need to talk about? This is what was so important?"

"No it's not that was just the question! What is so important is what I have to say next."

"Well what is it?"

"I had a doctor's appointment today."

"Yes, and?"

By this time Veronica's wonder had turned into rage she had gotten herself so worked up with her assumption that she didn't realize Isaac's mood changing.

"And I had some test done. Some test that I thought would surely keep my faith in you from faltering. But the test failed me! And so have you!"

"What? What do you mean so have I?"

"I have a secret that no one knows but me and my mother. Something that I wanted so bad to share with you but could never find the strength. It all started when I was sixteen. I fell in love and that love didn't sit to well with my mother at that time. She insisted that I was too young to feel that way about anyone especially not the young lady who the feelings were for. Her name was Sherita and we went to school together before I transferred to U of D Jesuit. Before that I attended Cass Technical High school and we were inseparable. Sherita was beautiful and smart but came from an unfortunate background. She was from a single parent home and constantly got into it with her mother until one day after a horrible fight her mother threw her out. With no other friends or family she was forced into a shelter. Never giving up she continued to go to school, but lost her way at some point. My mother never approved of our relationship and we were forced to sneak around to see each other. Well all that sneaking got us in more trouble than we could handle. Sherita was pregnant and the child was mine. My mother never believed her and assumed she was just blaming me to find a way out of her situation."

"So you're saying you have a baby momma running around that I never knew about? You have a child!"

"Please don't interrupt! Sherita carried the baby and delivered, but she would never leave the hospital. She died giving birth to a child. To my child and I could do nothing about it. I couldn't save her, and I blamed myself. If I had never got her pregnant she would still be here today. I never wanted to feel the way I did at that moment again! I never wanted to be the cause of someone else's pain again. My mother helped me and I admit she probably helped herself at the same time but we made it so that I would never feel that pain again. I had a minor surgery and it fixed my problem. I thought that with Sherita my chances at love died as well, but then I met you."

"A surgery what type of surgery?"

"I had an operation that doesn't allow me to have children, it's not the same as being clipped but it works. The only question is whether or not they came untied and that's where today's exams came in. I went in to find out if I am still unable to have children and the answer is yes! I'm still tied off and unable to produce a child. So how is it that you are pregnant that's the real question. I ignored what my own mother said for you, and I loved you! But above all else I trusted you and this is how you repay me?"

"I, I, I..........."

"There is nothing you can say to me! It's over between us Veronica!" My trust for you is over, and in turn so is this marriage!"

Veronica stood there in disbelief, dropping where she stood amazed and embarrassed at the same time. She wanted so badly to say something that would make this all go away, something that would make the entire problem go away, but there were no words that express how she felt. Definitely no words to make this situation any better. Falling to her knees, then curling up in the middle of the floor. She was beaten and battered, with no answers she wallowed in her own pity, and a pool of her own tears. As Isaac walked out of the house, and out of her life.

After the news given by his father Mark had a new outlook on life no longer did he have to live under the hefty weight of his father's shadow. He could finally be himself and make his own decisions, and the first one he decided to make was to be with Roslyn. He wouldn't let another day go by feeling guilty about being with another woman. He was seriously thinking of making his way to the job, but instead decided to call her cell there was no answer. Taking a quick glance at the clock in the car he decided to stop by the house for a quick shower. A couple quick turns and he was pulling into his drive-way immediately noticing his wife's car in the backyard. He wasn't in the mood to deal with her, and at the same time he wasn't prepared to play his leaving card just yet. As he approached the back door he looked into the window to his Amber holding the baby in the air starring at their beautiful baby girl. With every feature of him mixed with her mother's bright complexion, the sight was amazing and stopped Mark in his tracks. For the first time it seemed as if he actually realized what he may have to lose. He was blessed beyond belief; he had everything most people dreamed about right in front of him. He had a family who adored him, a wife that truly loved him unconditionally. No matter how he had treated her in the past she never gave up on him, she was there when no one else even attempted to care. The entire time he had been married he had been the worst version of himself, and for what? Amber had done nothing wrong throughout their entire relationship nothing but love a man that treated her like shit! The same man that was actually contemplating leaving her as she stood there with their child.

Mark turned the key, and walked into the house wondering what had come over him. As he stepped into the door he could feel what Amber immediately questioned him about.

"Mark what's wrong? Are you okay?"

With out so much as a word Mark walked over to his family snatching them both into his arms with tears flowing from his eyes. Amber was shocked and at a loss for words, she hadn't felt or seen this side of Mark since before the accident. She wondered what might've happened to bring this about. Though she had been waiting for this moment for as long as she could remember she couldn't help but wonder where it was coming from. She could feel the love from her husband and it was so strong that it brought tears to her eyes. They stood there all three intertwined with both parents' eyes full of tears holding on to each other for dear life. This was where he should be, where he needed, finally he realized this is where wanted to be. This was family, this was HOME! And if for any reason he was still even the least bit unsure Amber set it in stone and set his mind at ease with her simple words.

"Its okay baby you're home! This is home baby!"

As the plane landed there was a certain silence between Asia and Terrance, it had been that way since their little encounter. The rest of their trip was nothing more than a camera flash before they knew it the cool Fall air that Detroit had to offer was hitting them in their faces. Happy to be home both of them still had questions that they seemed too afraid to ask. Their minds racing a mile a minute as they wrestled with the right and wrong of their weekend adventure. The questions weren't so much about right and wrong as much as they were about if they were right for them. An even better question was what did this mean for their marriage?

Finally pulling up in the drive way, Asia sighed with relief "Home sweat home!" then with a quick glance at her husband she smiled. As Terrance looked back at his wife he realized that there was so much to their marriage than they had explored so far. Making a hasty decision they decided to leave the bags for later and go relax for a while. Their idea of relaxation just so happened to be in tuned with one another. At least until Asia placed her purse on the edge of the kitchen table, and it tipped over onto the floor. As they both tried to clean up the mess, Terrance ran across the business card of their third party.

"So what's this? When did you grab this?"

"What?"

"You know what Asia! Why did you grab this?"

"Terrance don't act surprised you probably mad I got to it before you!"

"What? You know that's not true! I was going to leave it right where it was."

"Yeah right not the way you were all up in her without hesitation! Did you even think twice before getting all up in that woman? Did you stop to think how I would feel?"

"What? I don't believe this! It's such a double standard! That place was your idea, not mine I didn't tell you I wanted to go to a swingers spot! What was I supposed to do just watch as another woman pleasured my wife? Did you stop to think about my feelings? How about how I would react? No you didn't so don't you dare stand there and try an put this all on me!"

The questions that had haunted them since the unbelievable night had finally come up. The why's and what's that had been silently thought were about to be vocalized. In Asia's mind she wondered if Terrance had been with other women since it was so easy for him to indulge right in her face. She also wondered what it was about Layla that excited him so much. Why was he so eager to be inside her? And most importantly why he lasted so long while pleasuring her. While Terrance questions were just as intriguing; what made her choose this place anyway? Has she always liked women? Had she been wanting this since they had been together and if so can he truly satisfy her?

They needed answers and the only person that they felt comfortable getting helped by was 700 miles away. Luckily they did have her business card with her telephone number. It wasn't until Terrance actually looked at the entire card that he realized why his wife kept it. Under her name he read her title.

Layla Chocolate
Sexual Relations Coach

They both wrestled with the idea of calling her after all she had been intimate with them there was no way she could be their therapist. They pondered for a couple hours before finally deciding to make the call. Unfortunately getting her voicemail, and not working up the nerve to leave a message they hoped the call was enough for her to get back to them.

Chapter 16: *Reality Bites*

Veronica sat on the floor of the living room eyes swollen, tears still running wondering where it all went wrong. How had she lost everything, her world was falling apart and it was all because of her whorish ways. She had no idea what she would do next, not only was she losing her husband but she was gaining a bastard child. Her life was turning into an episode of Maury, and she was the idiotic chick on stage not knowing who her baby daddy was. Her guilt didn't stop her from placing the blame somewhere else either. She couldn't be the only one at fault here, she refused to be. And she knew just who to blame for her situation but that wouldn't be easy. She would need more than just the hate, and contempt her mother-in-law had shown for her to truly blame her for this mishap.

Veronica still couldn't believe that her husband had a son. It was a huge pill to swallow, it was bigger than him having an operation and never telling her. Veronica decided to do one of the few other things she was good at besides sex. She started digging for information about the whole incident. Through her vast connections Veronica managed to find out the hospital in which the child was born. And before long she also had more information than she could've ever imagined! Finding out that one of her very good friends worked at the hospital in question she was able to give Veronica an entire background of the birth. The news was so incredible that Veronica decided to get up and pick up copies of the information for herself.

Thanks in part to the conversation that Mark had with his father, he seemed to be back to his senses. Even better was that he was not only back but better than he was before. He had a certain appreciation for what he had been blessed with. A beautiful wife, that was more understanding and loving than he could've ever imagined. They had a beautiful little girl that he would do anything in the world for, and she deserved a father that she could be proud of. Unfortunately Mark's mind was forever wondering, he was due back at work in the morning and he had no idea of what he planned to tell his boss. What was worse was he had no clue as to how she would react to his decision to break off their relationship. Even with his upcoming discussion, Mark had an even bigger decision to make. His guilt over his infidelity had become an increasing problem for him, since the conversation with his father he had been battling with himself. Wondering if he should try to forget the entire situation or should he simply come clean about everything. Mark questioned whether he could start over with his family without a clean slate, if he wasn't honest he would still be keeping secrets and that was no way to start over. Convincing himself that he should worry about one problem at a time he decided to leave this problem alone at least for now.

That night Mark and his family all slept in the same bed. With their daughter between them Mark and Amber slept facing each other. Hands entangled and locked as they dozed off into a beautiful slumber. Almost making it through the night Mark's dreams were haunted by the actions of his life. Waking him minutes before his clock was due to go off. Making sure not to wake his family, Mark got up turning the clock off before it sounded waking the two sleeping beauties that he was forced to leave this morning. Mark rose from the bed and headed for his shower and clothes in the basement of the house, trying his best to remember the just of the dream that woke him early. Walking past his phone as he headed for the shower Mark noticed he had missed a total of three messages. He had a voicemail, a text, and a picture message. Quickly opening the phone he realized that all the messages were from the same person. Roslyn had left a text, saying how much her and her friend missed him. Then if that wasn't enough she left a picture of herself naked, and finally the voicemail was of her moaning as she played with herself. It didn't seem like she was going to go away without a fight. Roslyn was going to make this decision extremely hard for him, but he knew that she wasn't worth his family.

If Mark thought he had the worst job on earth before just imagine what he had to look forward to today. He now had to work with the woman that had brought him to an entirely new sexual height and couldn't so much as brush up against her. On top of that he had to tell her it was over. At least he was back to his old self showing up to work just in time to start work. That should've been a sign, because for the couple of weeks that he and the boss were messing around he was there early. Walking in and going straight to the line, he refused to look up and acknowledge Roslyn as she stood in her usual place, before walking into her office. Mark managed to work the entire day without running into her, going as far as to have lunch in his truck so that he wouldn't bump into Roslyn during his time. Mark was nearly home free that was until it was quitting time. Just as he was getting into the car his phone rang and her car rode pass. Roslyn watched as Mark looked at the call, shook his head then sent it to voicemail. If she was just guessing earlier in the day she knew for a fact now. Mark was ignoring her, the only thing she needed to know now is why! That didn't stop her from leaving a message for him.

"Look it's obvious you are having some kind of issue and are avoiding me. I don't know what your problem is but know this! If you are trying to break it off with me it's no big deal! I knew the situation when we started, you aren't the first and you definitely won't be the last! The least you could've done was be a man about it!"

Mark was alerted about the voicemail just before he arrived at home. Pulling into the drive-way he decided that he would listen before going in the house. After listening to the message he was sure he was in the clear. He wouldn't have to deal with the awkwardness of breaking it off with Roslyn she already knew what was going on. It was true that he seemed to be taking the cowards way out but who cares as long as it's over.

Two days had passed since returning back home from their trip and Asia and Terrance still hadn't heard from their friend. Though tension had died down tremendously in their household, things weren't so good that the couple didn't need help. Neither of them were looking forward to the upcoming weekend, and being off of work at the same time. Deciding that once wasn't enough Asia called the number on the card once more, but this time being sure to leave a message for their coach. While on the phone Asia also decided that since the Fall was coming to an end and the weather wasn't horrible just yet. She wanted to end it right, a cookout was just what the doctor ordered. Terrance was always at his best while entertaining and this would be a great time to have the girls from church over. After all they had enjoyed each other so much since they planned the event, she thought they might as well keep the friendship going. After leaving her message, she hung up her phone and then texted her husband to tell him about her great idea.

It didn't take much convincing to get Terrance on board with the idea. It was as if the two had the same thought process. Not only was it a good way to end the season, it was also a way to keep them from tearing each other apart with questions. Terrance had a couple people that he wanted to invite from work, and of course he would invite his nephew Chris as well. There was no better way to thank him for being a guest speaker than to feed him for free. Plus that would give Terrance a chance to talk him into coming to church on Sunday. Something Terrance had been trying to do as long as he could remember. Chris seemed to be a busy man since becoming a journalist, he was always on the go. Add that to Chris not being a regular church participant anyway and you had the perfect equation for someone who was going to try his best not to be there. Food was a totally different story! One quick call and the mention of his uncles famous ribs was just about all it took to seal Chris's presence at the party. One last question was on Chris's mind.

"Unk are there going to be any availables at this party?"

"Well I'm not sure but I'll see what we can do about that!"

Terrance knew that between him and Asia's single friends that he would definitely have a couple of women there to keep his nephew's attention. He would also invite a couple of women from the hospital, that way he could invite the new nurses as well. Most of them would love a chance to visit his home, and since he knew he couldn't so much as touch them why not keep it in the family. That is if Chris was up to the task.

Asia had the E-vites ready and out quickly, the weekend came even quicker. Terrance was out preparing early Saturday morning coming straight home from work and beginning the preparation of the yard for this afternoon. He had spent most of his time at work this week inviting people to this weekend's shin ding. Making sure to invite the sexiest women the hospitals had to offer. Asia invited Veronica, and Amber as well as their husbands along with a host of other individuals. The party was going to be packed with friends and family coming from far and wide to enjoy this backyard barbecue.

Amber had every intention of being there with Mark, and the new Mark was happy to please his wife. He had completed a full circle, now instead of avoiding his wife at all cost, Mark wanted to spend as much time with her as possible. With good reasoning, Mark knew that idle time was the devil's playground. Understanding that temptation was something he didn't have complete control over. He wanted desperately to cut down on the possibilities, and he couldn't think of a better way than to stick close to his wife's side.

Veronica had an all together different problem, Isaac wasn't even coming home. Let alone showing his face to some friendly function. She was afraid that she was in the midst of losing her husband though this wasn't something that Veronica was ready to let everyone in on. She was pretty sure the marriage was over, but she still held on to a glimmer of hope. Maybe Isaac would somehow find it in his heart to forgive her. Maybe he would give her another chance, maybe he could find it in his heart to love her again. Lightening was more likely to strike in the same place twice, but we all have hopes and dreams.

The end of the week had a way of sneaking up on people and this weekend was no different. Before Terrance knew what hit him Saturday was here and the party was on. Up and at it, near the crack of dawn he knew he had a lot of work to do to get ready for the guests. Luckily the yard men were able to move them up on the schedule, so the grass had been cut and trimmed Friday afternoon. Asia insisted that her husband get an early start on the barbecuing because she refused to be stuck being the host while he just sat in front of the grill the whole time. Terrance had made it up in his mind that him in front of the pit was him being a good host and couldn't understand how his wife didn't agree. Making sure the yard was set up to accommodate their guest, Terrance turned his attention to making his famous fire, which usually consisted of overdosing the coals with lighter fluid and coming as close to the singeing of his eye brows as possible without having an accident. Afterward he would always feel as if he was one of the first cave men and the fire was actually his invention. Just as it was good and ready and had been burning for a good thirty minutes Terrance went back into the house and pulled out the ribs. He was very protective of his secret recipe. He kept it well guarded, a lot of times it seemed as if he was keeping the secret of who shot JFK. The meat had been marinating through the night, allowing the juices to soak in completely through to the bone. Terrance had a certain knack for making barbecue, and nothing was off limits. From ribs and franks, to sausages, and chicken. Terrance could do it all, he pulled out the shrimp kabobs, and even a salmon fillet. He was in rare form by noon. Happy he did decide to get an early start because by that time he was hot and bothered. The event just happened to be on the last warm day Detroit would see for a long time. By the time 12:30 hit it was already up to 62 degrees and still climbing. Not even twenty minutes later the early birds were starting to roll in. You always had one set of friends who not only refused to operate on CP time, but they took the extra incentive to actually be early. Lucky for Asia their early guests were Amber and Mark, and the young couple was eager to help with getting everything ready.

Mark and Amber happily helped with the last minute set ups, in between them being unbelievably affectionate with one another. It was as if Amber couldn't complete any one task without Mark throwing his arms around her and stealing a kiss or just a touch. Mark usually took the time to put on a show in front of friends and family but it would be nothing like this. When he was faking it, the most he could do was say kind words and if he really wanted to sell it maybe even a kiss on the cheek. But nothing like this, it was as if he was a totally different person. Amber wasn't bothered in the least, she was too busy loving every waking second of the blissful feeling that his action invoked. His action had Amber feeling loved and desirable for the first time since high school.

The more time that went by the more people showed, until there was a steady flow into the back yard and the house. Terrance entertained while Asia took forever and a day to get dressed for the event. Having to go with a totally different outfit than the one she picked for today's event. The weather was too nice for what she had in mind, but knowing Asia she would be changing again before the night was over. Finally she made her descent downstairs to the party, looking absolutely fabulous. Just in time too, because whether she was downstairs or not Terrance was on his way up. He was tired of talking to people with sauce all over his shirt and smelling like an open pit. As they passed each other at the back door Terrance seriously thought about grabbing his wife and pulling her into his shirt, but thought better of it not wanting to deal with the repercussions. Though he did think it might have been worth it for the laugh. Asia had absolutely no problem taking over as the life of the party she smiled and chatted everyone up. Making sure everyone had a plate or a cup, she was in top hostess form tonight, and the night just started. As she stood in the backyard laughing and joking she noticed the White Lexus Land Rover pull up with the exquisite golden trim. Knowing exactly who it was a smile came across Asia's face. Thinking to herself "Damn some people gonna be late to their own funeral!" Veronica slowly exited the over sized truck looking all too stunning for a simple backyard party. Looking as if she had a gala to attend following tonight's festivities. Closing her car door behind her and hitting the alarm there was no sign of her husband being anywhere behind her. Excusing herself from the conversation she was a part of, Asia made her way over to Veronica to greet her new favorite friend. Not wasting a second of her time she immediately went in for the kill.

"Umm V! Where is that husband of yours?"

"Girl you know I can't keep up with that man."

As Veronica paused for just a second to see if her explanation would be sufficient, both women chuckled and laughed.

"I know exactly what you mean if I didn't have a leash on Terrance I couldn't keep up with him either."

"I know that's right! No but seriously he is at the office working as usual. I told him he is going to work himself to death before it's all said and done."

"Well at least it's better than the alternative. We should be thankful to have hard working men in our life as bad as it is for people out here in today's society."

"Mmmm hmmm! I told him about today and he said if he got done early enough he would definitely stop by."

"Well that's just fine. Let's get you a plate and a place to sit. I wanna introduce you to a couple people too so hurry up and get comfortable."

"Yes ma'am!"

Veronica found herself a comfortable area and made a small portioned plate. She decided to sit at a table full of women, knowing she didn't want to even come near a man with her current situations. Noticing a couple members of the church scattered throughout the crowd. Veronica hoped and prayed to herself that she wouldn't be running into Mrs. Patton-Silver on this day. Putting her mind at ease was the fact that the crowd was a bit on the younger side. Even the people from the church who decided to show up were some of the younger members. So more than likely that meant that Veronica at least had one more day where she didn't have to hear or see Mrs. Patton-Silver, and wouldn't have to have her name dragged through the mud.

While Terrance was in the house throwing together an outfit, he heard the phone ringing. Rushing over to the phone while still attempting to get his pants pulled up and buttoned. Fumbling with the phone at the same time he finally got it to his ear.

"Hello? Uh hello! Is anyone there hello."

Finally the voice at the other end of the phone responded. In a low and sexy tone.

"Hello? Can you hear me now?"

"Yes I can here you."

"Sorry about you not hearing me before my phone must be in a bad connection area. Is Asia available?"

"Unfortunately not right this second she is outside may I take a message?"

"Well, is this Terrance?"

"Yes this is. May I ask who I'm speaking to?"

"Well of course you can! This is Layla, and I'm on my way from the airport. I mistakenly misplaced the directions to the house do you think you could walk me through them? Better yet just give me the address and I'll put it in my navigation system."

"Layla? Layla from Georgia Layla?"

"The one and only Suga!"

After running down the address and even telling her the quickest way to the house. Terrance fell back on the bed in a daze. "Why the hell was she here, and why didn't Asia tell me she was coming?" Time was steadily ticking as Terrance mentally tried to pull himself together. Finally leaving the upstairs of the house he made it back down to the party just in time to see Christopher as he entered the gate.

Coming in wasting no time making sure to do as little meeting and greeting as possible. Making a B-line for the food tent that was set up. Chris had nose for his uncle's barbeque to be honest it was between that and his grandmother's sweet potato pie. Anytime either of the two foods were around, it was as if his stomach spoke directly to him and nothing else could be heard. Just as he made it to the tent he was intercepted by his aunt and her persistence. She had people that she wanted her successful nephew to meet. Whispered to him that some of the women are involved, but none of them were married. Asia had been trying to set Chris up with a good and wholesome church going God fearing woman for the last couple of years to no avail. Chris had no intent on settling down especially not with one of her good and wholesome lady friends. He was only interested if they were a little less wholesome, but were looking to hoe some. According to Chris women didn't have a shot of settling him down, especially not after the last two women he had been serious about, but to satisfy his aunt he would at least meet them.

As the two of the made their way through the back yard doing the meet and greet thing. Chris noticed the beautiful woman sitting amongst a crowd of women nudging his aunt attempting to get her attention he whispered.

"Who is that?"

"Who?"

"Over there sitting with the other chicks!"

"Umm that really narrows it down, Christopher! That table is full of women!"

"Yeah Auntie but only one of them, is worth talking about."

Worried that Chris had targeted Veronica, Asia attempted to break his concentration but knew that it was a waste of time. She used the only thing she could think of to turn him off. "Oh, that's Veronica her husband just left they both go to our church." A well timed, well thought out response was all it took. Chris took one more glance, and then quickly lost interest. Terrance stepped in explaining to his wife that he needed to speak to her. His interruption was in the nick of time. Chris's stomach had taken over and he could barely hear anything his aunt had to say anymore. He quickly turned and headed back to the tent to grab a serving of his favorite foods.

While Chris was hell bent on feeding face his uncle was looking to feed his curiosity. He wanted to know why exactly the rule of what happens in Atlanta stays in Atlanta was being broken. Why on earth would his wife had invited their fling to their home? What was even more important was why she hadn't taken the time to even ask him how he felt about the idea. Quickly reminding his better half that moves like that is what had them in their current situation in the first place. Asia had a simple and direct answer, and whether Terrance liked the answer or not he had to accept it. Besides them having questions that still needed to be answered, Asia also thought that Layla was going to be able to help them in other areas of their marriage that truly could use her touch.

"Terrance this will be good for the both of us, but this is a discussion that we will have later tonight. We still have guest to entertain."

Before he could get his response out his wife had turned and began to walk away.

While fixing an enormous plate of food Chris finally discovered something that peeked his interest without the hardware placed on the fourth finger of her left hand. She was absolutely beautiful. Even though she had the muscle tone of a WNBA player, which had become a serious turn off for Chris since an earlier encounter in life. She was standing near the tent holding a conversation that she really didn't want to be having. One of his uncle's doctor friends was pulling out all the stops trying to hold her attention. She stood there as if she was stuck, being bored to death. Chris thought about going over to save her from boredom but thought better of it as he watched the club like scene. There were guys waiting in the wings hoping to snag her as soon as the dear doctor stepped away. That's never a good situation, it's enough to have the most down to earth woman make a turn for the worst. Chris continued to eat, but kept a close eye out for a possible opportunity. As he watched carefully not to be seen by anyone else, he was interrupted by his uncle.

"Hey Unk!"

"How are you Chris?"

"Been better, been worse so I guess I'm okay! How about you?"

"It's a beautiful day, and I have friends and family here to celebrate that with. I'm great."

"Is that right? Well I'll tell you what's great! These ribs! You did it again Unk! When are you going to let me in on that secret sauce of yours?"

"Now you know I can't do that! If I tell you that how will I convince you to do the things I want you to do?"

"Good point I guess you have to keep this one to yourself."

"Yeah I think so!"

"So is it enough eye candy here for you?"

"Well, there are a couple treats!"

"We gotta find you someone who can get you to settle down."

"Not you too! You know your wife was out here with that same lecture, and agenda. I guess it's true what they say!"

"Oh really? And what is it that they say?"

"Misery loves company!"

With a huge smile both men stood there and laughed. Chris took the opportunity to inquire about the beautiful woman who was being harassed by just about every so called gentleman in the yard. After pointing her out making sure it wasn't too obvious, Chris got what he refused to go and get, her name.

"That young lady's name is Roslyn."

One of the guys that Christopher had noticed scoping Roslyn wasn't looking in the manner Chris might have thought. This individual was looking on in terror! Mark had absolutely no idea what Roslyn was doing there, but like most men immediately thought that it had something to do with him. A man's ego undoubtedly has the ability to be his biggest down fall. The truth was Roslyn had been invited by Terrance, and furthermore had no idea she would be running into Mark at this function. How was she supposed to know that they attended the same church! Though she had noticed Mark, she had no intent on speaking to him. She didn't want to make him anymore uncomfortable than he obviously already was. But while she had no intention on making things worse, she didn't plan on making them any better either. She would make him sweat! After all he wasn't even man enough to break their secret off in person! He deserved to sweat at least this time.

Sweating was exactly what Mark was doing, trying his best not to allow his anxiety to be detected by his wife. Mark became more and more fidgety the longer he and Amber sat there. The only thing he could think of to get him a breath of fresh air was a trip to the bathroom. Excusing himself from the table, he headed straight for the house. Almost to the state of hyperventilation, Mark rushed in the bathroom splashing his face with water trying his best to calm down. Mumbling to himself, hoping and praying that this was nothing more than a coincidence. Going back and forth with himself wondering if he should approach her some how, or if he should just leave. Finally he came to his senses, she had to be invited after all it was a possibility that she worked at the hospital, or was studying there. There had to be a logical explanation for her being there. An explanation that had nothing to do with him!

Just as Mark had calmed himself and headed back outside he caught a glimpse of something that just about brought tears to his eyes. Though Roslyn had decided not to approach Mark, she thought she would make him sweat even more! Sitting between Amber and Veronica, Roslyn was harmlessly holding a conversation with the two women. It was more so to get a break from the constant onslaught by the men at the party. Mark stepped back into the house backing up into Terrance and Chris. Startled and overwhelmed he quickly pulled himself together.

"Hey Mark! Good to see you! I want you to meet my nephew. Mark Coleman this is Christopher Alexander."

"Hey Chris! I remember you from my father's birthday event. I wanted to thank you for speaking so highly of him."

"No problem Mark it was my pleasure! Your father is a great man!"

"Thank you! I'm sure he would love to thank you himself! Will you be able to make it to service tomorrow?"

"Ummm, well I...."

Chris tried to search his mind for a good excuse as to why he couldn't make it. He noticed out of the corner of his eye the look Terrance was giving him. Taking that look into consideration before he finished his answer Chris accepted the offer though he wasn't happy about it at all. Chris couldn't help but think to himself that he should've definitely eaten and run.

Terrance noticed a new car pulling up and looking as if it was searching for a parking spot. Assuming it was Layla he stepped back out side and walked to the street. Still not completely sure of what the hell was going on he made his way to the car. Sure enough it was Layla looking as though she was lost even with the house being right in front of her. Terrance tapped on her window, and startled the beautiful woman.

"Looking for us?"

"Why yes sir I do believe I am."

Terrance walked to the end of the back yard and opened the gate allowing their guest to pull into the drive-way. Asia noticed who it was and excused herself from a conversation she was having with the girls. Walking down to them both with a huge smile on her face. After all this was the only woman who had ever pleasured her before, she was definitely happy to see her.

"Hey! I'm glad you could make it!"

"Of course Asia, I wouldn't miss it for the world. Thank you for the invite."

"Girl hush! You're more than welcome!"

"Well how was the flight? Was the seat okay?"

"Yes it was when you said you were going to get me a ticket, I never had a clue that you would be buying me a first class flight! I almost wish the flight was longer so I could enjoy the entire first class experience."

"Well I'm glad you enjoyed the flight. Come on let me introduce you to a couple of our friends and family."

The threesome walked through the crowd introducing while laughing and joking throughout. Introducing their guest to just about everyone who made it to today's event. Though time was getting short Layla had finally arrived towards the end of the event people had been there for such a long time, and most of them had already done what they came to do. We know how our people can be after they eat good they get a case of the "Itise", so as Layla was just getting comfortable a lot of the guest were getting ready to hit the road. The only people who were left were Chris, Roslyn, Veronica, Amber, and Mark with a couple scattered guests making to go plates. Considering the Fall weather was upon them and though the day had been kind and full of the suns warmth. The cool night air began to sneak in forcing the party from outside to indoors. But before he was to be trapped in the house talking about current events and life Mark convinced Amber that he too had fell victim to the "Itise" and they prepared to go home.

That left the group down to just the six of them. In any other situation Chris would've been gone without a second thought but this was different. He saw something he liked and it was no longer just Roslyn, and Veronica. Layla did something to him as well, and for him that was different. He rarely went for the deep dark chocolate but she was unmistakable. She was the essence of beauty, and had acquired his attention without even trying. Though she hadn't acquired his complete attention, she did have some. Asia and Terrance were about ready to clear the house out and get down to a long awaited conversation. Neither of them wanted it to seem to obvious, but they were no longer in the mood to play host. After all it had been a long day!

Less than thirty minutes had past, before Roslyn felt that she had over stayed her welcome. Looking around the room it seemed as if she was the odd one out. Everyone that was left were either family or close friends, at least that's how it seemed to her. She concluded it was time to make her way home as she said her Good-Bye's. Chris insisted on walking her to her car.

"Well you know you don't have to walk me to my car it's right across the street."

"What kind of gentlemen would I be if I didn't?"

"Well I'm a big girl that can take care of herself!"

"Yes! I can see the grown woman all up and through you! And I'm sure you can handle yourself in any position.......I mean any situation."

"Hmm... I bet that's what you meant!"

"So Roslyn are you going to let me call you? Or am I not worthy of that pleasure?"

"Well as far as you being worthy, I don't know that you are but I'll give you a chance anyway. Here's my number!"

"Wow! So can I assume you already planned on giving me your number before I asked? Or should I assume that you have been passing your number out all day?"

"You can assume whatever you like, but you know what they said assuming does! If you have issues with taking the number give it back."

"No I think I can handle it! I was just thinking that if you don't have any plans for tomorrow, I have to attend this event and I would love it if you escorted me. What do you think?"

"Depends, on how early. I'm not much of a morning person when I don't have to be."

"That works for me, lucky for us the event starts around three this week."

"Well 3:00 sounds doable, but it depends on what I do for the rest of the night."

With that Roslyn closed her car door and put her car in drive Chris insisted that she rolled her window down so he could tell her to give him a call once she makes it home. He wanted to make sure she was safe tonight. With a devilish smile Roslyn agreed then pulled off. Chris thought about going back in the house for a second, but choose to go another route instead. He was feeling a bit run down and wasn't in the mood to deal with family anymore, especially when he had to be with them at church tomorrow. Chris made a quick call into the house to let his uncle know that he was leaving. Terrance asked him to wait just a second because Veronica was on her way out and he wanted to make sure she made it to her car safely. Chris waited on the beautiful married woman, then walked her to her car. Making sure she made it safely to her car, he thought about saying something to her but let the thought pass. She looked troubled as if she had a lot on her mind and for once he didn't want to add to a woman's troubles. While Veronica's night was over Chris's night was just beginning or so he hoped. As far as Terrance, Asia, and Layla went they had a long night in front of themselves.

Chapter 17: *Dusk before the Dawn*

Mark had a long night ahead of him struggling with the battle raging on inside. The battle of confessions! Mentally waging war with his mind and his heart. Mark's heart heavy, with hurt and pain that he had caused the mother of his child. The sleepless night's the evil ways. He had done so much in oh so little time, and on top of it all he had been unfaithful. Not only to her, but also to his daughter neither of which had done anything except love and cherish him. He had also been untrue in his eyes to God, after all there had been a ceremony that took place before all. Mark's heart and his faith told him to confess his sins so that they may be washed and he may be forgiven, but his mind thought otherwise! In his mind he thought after all she had dealt with after all he had put her through she did not deserve the hurt of this truth. His rationale seemed a bit as if he was saving himself the torment of having to tell her. Saving himself the torment of having to deal with her decision. Would she leave or would she stay?

His night was a constant battle between his heart and conscience versus his mind and reasoning. His heart and conscience arguing that she deserves to know, and how guilty they feel about what they had done.

While his mind and reasoning argued that the guilt is the exact reason they need to keep this to themselves. The war of words went on for hours deep into the night.

"We have to tell her! It's the only way we can move on in our relationship! Besides it would be devastating for her to find out from someone besides us!"

"You idiots! We made a mistake a mistake that we made alone. A one time mistake that we learned from and will never make again. It makes no since to burden her with a burden that we should be taking on ourselves."

"That's where you're wrong she deserves to know. We can't take a decision as big as this away from her. That would be wrong of us! The guilt will take over it will worry us to death, constantly worrying about if she knows something or not!"

"That is just us being selfish! It will never happen again why should we destroy what we have? Destroy our family because we can't handle the guilt! This is a burden that we are destined to carry to our graves. Not only do we owe it to her for all the bullshit we have put her through but for that beautiful little girl that we have as well."

"What kind of husband, father, better yet what kind of man would we be if we held on to something this important?"

"We would be a good man! The man that cares more about his family and their wellbeing than his own! The kind of man that our father raised us to be we have no choice but to keep this to ourselves! We and we alone should suffer this torment."

Mark was convinced that the good outweigh the bad and his mind won the battle, but only time would tell if his guilty heart would win the war. Finally getting ready for bed and a long day at church tomorrow he finally allowed his eyes to close and sleep to ease his mind. Rolling over and pulling Amber closer to him as he dosed off for the night.

Veronica on the other hand had a much different night in store stuck in a place no person should be. Just as Mark was she was filled with guilt, but unlike him she found a way to blame everyone else but herself. Still hell bent on taking revenge on Mrs. Patton-Silver she had all the proof she needed to make her life a living hell. She would exact her revenge soon! There was absolutely no way she would allow her to steal away her marriage and get away with it. The family secret was now going to be up for public debate, and her motives would be in question.

Veronica was hoping that the questions coming from more than just her would be enough to get her husband to at least question his mother.

Her husband hadn't been back home since the confrontation, Veronica had come to the conclusion that he was staying with his mother. Which infuriated her even more, unfortunately she would have to deal with it. She hadn't heard so much as a peep from Isaac, and could only hope that he would be in church tomorrow.

Isaac refused to bring his mother into the fold, he had turned his cell off when he left the house days ago. Having no intent on turning it back on anytime soon because he didn't need the continuous calls from Veronica. As far as hearing I told you so from his mother, he was definitely in no mood for that. Plus he still had two huge and final decisions to make. One seemed more important than the other at the time but the truth was they were of equal importance. He never felt the way he felt about Veronica before, even with her infidelity she was still the love of his life. He needed to know if he could ever forgive her, and if this was something that they might be able to work through. His mind said there was no way in hell that he could ever take her back, but in his heart he knew that anything was possible. Especially if the Lord was involved after all Isaac still loved his Veronica. Tomorrow would be a great indication of it all tonight's prayer was for spiritual guidance. He needed God's guidance in making not only the decision about his marriage, but also in regard to his son.

"Dear Lord: I know I don't do everything that I should do and I know that I don't thank you enough. But Lord I need your guidance in my life! I have decisions in my life that I need your help to make. Lord I've tried it my way and now I need you to take control and show me the right way and now I know Lord the right way is your way. Please Lord can you please give me a SIGN! Just something I can recognize as your truth."

With his prayer done Isaac climbed into the hotel bed that he had made his home away from home since he left his wife. Another night starring at an unfamiliar ceiling in a dwelling he had become all too familiar with. He wanted to be home!

Roslyn made it home rather quickly a little upset about the beginning of the party, but excited at the possibilities towards the end. After all she had met Christopher there, and that in itself may have been more than enough to go through seeing Mark with his wife. Add to that how it looked as if Mark was going to shit his pants seeing her there. Today wasn't so bad after all, and tonight might just prove to be even better. She kept her promise calling Chris as she settled in for the night. Even with Mark being an asshole, and a coward he still had the ability to get her a little hot. A night cap was just what the doctor ordered and she had a good idea of who she wanted to get it from. She thought about calling after her shower but with a guy like Christopher she knew she didn't have all night. If she didn't act quickly he would be into something or someone else. Roslyn grabbed her cell, hitting the buttons, getting directly to her missed calls, then sending the call to Chris hoping he was available. Four rings later he picked up music blasting in the background. With an inflection in his voice he responded over the music.

"Hold on a sec!"

Roslyn hoped he was reaching over to turn the music down a bit. So she could hear his voice over the phone. She was happy when she could barely hear the sweat voice of J. Holiday singing his hit "Bed". She realized at that moment that she had called just in time. He was listening to mood music, she had to work fast. More than likely Chris had already made plans for the rest of his night. The idea now was to change those plans, but that would be the easy part.

"Hey I'm back who is this?"

"Well I'll let you guess on that one, but I will give you a hint. You told me to let you know when I made it home."

"Wow! Roslyn......this is a surprise, I really didn't expect to hear your voice tonight."

"Well I just wanted to let you know I made it home safely. I hope I'm not interrupting anything or getting you in any trouble."

"That was really cute! Was that a gauging question? No sweetheart you are not getting me in any trouble and you're not interrupting anything. I'm free right now I was on my way.........um home."

"What do you mean was that a gauging question, and why the pause before you say you're going home?"

"You know what a gauging question is! One of those questions you ask for more than the answer at hand. That was a subtle way of asking me if I was with my women or with someone else.......a gauging question. And I didn't realize I paused before saying I was going home."

"Well you did!"

"Well I'm sure you had a purpose in asking me if you were interrupting. Am I right? Did you have anything particular in mind?"

"No I was just making sure."

"Is that right? Well you didn't strike me as the shy type but hey I can't always be right."

"I'm not shy!"

"Then tell me the truth! Is there something else that we should be discussing right now or did you only call to let me know you made it home?"

"That's all unless you have something to say."

"Nope not at all! Well thanks for letting me know I'll see you tomorrow right?"

"Yeah I guess so! Only because you want to wait until tomorrow!"

"Well I didn't know I had a different option. Are you saying I have a different option?"

"Chris would you like to come over and keep me warm tonight?"

"Now that's the Roslyn I thought I met today! The straight forward grown woman! That's what I like!"

"Well if that's the case come show me how much you like it!"

"My pleasure address please?"

"I'm in Southfield in Sutton Place just call me when you get to the gate."

"Be there in fifteen minutes!"

They both hung up their phones looking forward to tonight's festivities. A quick pit stop for a protection box and Mr. Alexander was on his way to another one of his rendezvous.

The house was quiet as the three of them sat there deciding who would start the conversation off. Layla decided to cut the tension, and at the same time get them a little more comfortable with the idea of her consoling them. Stating that she could understand that this may be an uncomfortable situation, but that they were all adults. That was about all that the couple needed, well if not the couple definitely Asia.

"Well it still is extremely hard for me to believe that we indulged in something like we did that night. Even harder to believe was Terrance actually having sex with some else!"

Terrance instantly looked up from the floor with an expression that could only be described by actually seeing it. He didn't believe he was getting the blame for the situation. It wasn't his idea and Asia had the nerve to be appalled by his actions.

"So it finally comes out! I couldn't believe that you took me to such a place. Don't try to twist this up you put me in the situation, and on top of it you started the party yourself! I couldn't believe that my wife was kissing another woman. Not only did you kiss her but you allowed her to do things that I would've never thought you would do!"

"Wait, wait, wait a minute you guys! Now you both have valid points the key is having a healthy discussion about your feelings. We are not here to place blame on either party. You guys have experienced something that few couples have had the ability to experience. Now we may not have gotten there the proper way, but it's not something that has to ruin your marriage.

First we have to find out how and why you ended up there, and the only way we can accomplish that is with open communication."

Asia and Terrance sat back in their seats attempting to calm themselves down. Layla was right, there was only one way for them to work this problem out. They realized that there was something missing in their marriage and that they both received something different from their encounter at the club. Layla continued with her speech and decided to start with Asia, she wanted to find out what made Asia want the adventure in the first place. According to Asia it was simply her curiosity getting the best of her. She had heard friends talking about their visit, and how much they enjoyed it. Most of the friends who chose to visit didn't attend with their husbands. That was the deciding factor for Asia and the one thing that kept her from going. She had no desire to indulge without her husband. What she didn't add to her explanation was that her hope was to get Terrance some sexual advice. She took him to the club so that he might get some pointers in the sexual department. She never intended on participating in a sexual encounter to just enjoy viewing them.

Layla took the time to interrupt changing the direction just a bit. She now wanted to know how Terrance felt once he realized where they were. Terrance not sure of how to answer the question constantly worried about the reaction of his wife. Attempting to ease the despair that showed so intensely on his face.

"Terrance understand that we are here for the betterment of your marriage. Not to place blame! You can feel comfortable answering the questions."

"Layla that sounds beautiful and would sound much better coming from my wife."

With a smile Asia explained that it was all going to be alright, and Terrance had nothing to worry about. Terrance returned the smile, then went into his description of the night. He made sure to mention that he was undoubtedly surprised by them being there. Though he didn't see it as a bad thing. Terrance went into the fact that their schedules don't leave much time for sexual pleasures. It had been that way ever since they met, well not ever since they met he could still remember early on in their relationship when they had a very healthy sex life. When they would go for hours just enjoy and indulging in each other. Unfortunately their indulgence allowed other parts of their lives to suffer namely their grades, and pursuits of career greatness. Something neither of them could imagine happening. After they both noticed the correlation between their sex life and their grades everything changed. At the time it seemed that it was for the best, they both graduated top of their class and started very great careers. Each climbing to new heights in their career, and spending less and less time worrying about the rest of their lives. There sex life became a flash in the pan, the quicker the better, after all they had more important things to do with their time. As Terrance's words continued to take both Layla and Asia on a trip down memory lane, Asia started to remember certain events that she had truly forgot about. Remembering how wild and freaky they use to be, how her then boyfriend use to make her squirm with the slightest touch. It had been so long that she had clearly forgot about it, she was so use to getting two minutes of pleasure that she forgot how much more he could do.

That explained all sorts of things and one of Asia's main questions! How the hell he was able to pleasure Layla the way he did? Though it didn't explain why he thought it was okay to do her in the first place! Layla could see the intrigue etched across the face of her female client.

"So Asia does your husband's story sound about right?"

"Actually it does! I can remember when our sex life was wild and exciting. Back then we couldn't keep our hands off each other!"

"Well this is my next question Asia! Does Terrance satisfy you sexually now?"

The question transferred the look of despair that her husband had earlier on to Asia. Not wanting to go through the entire speech again, Layla merely threw out a quick phrase to bring the answer out of Asia.

"It's okay take your time."

"Well it's not that he doesn't, it's just that it..........."

"It's what Asia? It's okay go ahead it will be okay, just say it."

"It doesn't........It doesn't......It's just doesn't last long enough. I was wondering how it was that he was able to keep it going with you so long. But when it comes to me it's over so quickly. I just don't understand."

With an embarrassed look on his face Terrance apologized to his wife.

"There is nothing for you to be sorry about Terrance, and Asia there are so many reasons that he was able to last so long with me. Starting with the fact that he thinks yours is so much better! Sex isn't just physical, it's mental and emotional as well. You can control each aspect, but if you lose control of anyone of them you can lose yourself sooner than you are ready to. Terrance may have been able to control them all with me because there was no mental, or emotional connection between us. So physically he was able to make it last. Another possibility is that you were unable to control your muscles. Then you have the possibility that he has become accustom to everything being quick. Every situation has the ability to be fixed, so now we just need to find out which one it is.

"So how do we do that?"

"Well there are many ways we can test the theories. The questions is what are you all willing to do to get the answers?"

The couple looked at each other then almost in unisons they replied. "Anything!"

Layla smiled then replied "Well we are in good shape then! We can start with just a few more questions. The questions continued for the next hour with a wide span covering all aspects of their lives, with suggestions on things that need to change from Layla as well as the couple. Before the discussion they both had come to the agreement that their encounter was not only a good idea, but had been a healthy outreach after all it did lead them to meet Layla.

Before they were allowed to go to bed Layla had a couple questions that she wanted answered for her own benefit. She turned her attention to Asia, and calmly asked a simple question.

"Did you allow me to enjoy you for you husband's sake or were you curious about women yourself? Don't answer that just yet! Terrance how did watching me taste your wife the way I did make you feel? Did you enjoy it? Don't answer that either! At least not yet I want you both to sleep on that, and answer me tomorrow. Feel free to discuss it amongst yourselves."

Once again the couple looked at each other wondering what the answers would be between the two of them. Layla explained that they were done for the night, and how she was suffering from a bit of jet lag. Not that it was honestly jetlag more than it was that time had flown by. It was a bit past 1:00am by now and she was beat. Asia agreed to show Layla to the guest room while Terrance ran out to the rental and grabbed their guest's overnight bag. The discussion had done both Terrance and Asia some good, each of them had a better understanding of the other's wants and needs not only in the sexual department. The open line of communication that they had established was one that could be used throughout their marriage. After making sure their guest was comfortable Asia and Terrance made their way back to their bedroom with plans of making each other more comfortable before bed.

As they entered the bedroom it was as if a switch had been hit they both completely forgot about their company. Terrance grabbed Asia's arm spinning her around to face him looking her deep in her eyes, then leaned in and gave her every ounce of passion in the first kiss. Asia couldn't remember the last time, her husband had done this. It was as if the kiss lit a fire deep inside her as she returned his passion. As they stood in between the dresser and the bed the couple couldn't decide which way they wanted to go next. Finally breaking their embrace Terrance asked his wife to hold on for just a second, breaking away walking into the master bath and turning on their shower room. Their shower doubled as a steam room and Terrance planned to take advantage of all the room it had tonight. Asia heard the water turn on, and just as she began to think her husband had ruined the mood yet again Terrance returned with nothing more than a towel wrapped around his waist. Asia smiled thinking to herself "How wrong was I!" she stood there for a second to enjoy the magnificent view of her husband as he came closer. She raised her hands attempting to unbutton herself, but her hands were gently slapped away. Terrance explained that was a job for him tonight, as he seductively undressed his beautiful wife. Taking the time to step back and enjoy the view of her naked body. Her workout regimen speaking for itself, as she stood there with nothing to hide behind. Grabbing her hand he lead her to the shower room, the steam had already began to form. The warmth of the beads of water pleasantly massaged their bodies, though the heat took a little getting use to. Terrance rubbed and caressed her beautiful body just right as he prepared her for a night of immense passion. Pressing her against the shower room wall, she felt the icy touch of the walls that had yet to soak in the heat of the room. Asia flinch ever so slightly, but the chill from the wall became a distant memory once her husband knelt and positioned himself between her golden arches. Placing her legs over his shoulders so that he was now face to face with the set of lips that had been neglected for way too long during this marriage. As he devoured the only meal that his barbeque couldn't compete with Asia's eyes rolled back as she clutched her husbands head like never before! Her hips began to gyrate as if she was in Jamaica listening to a bit of reggae music. She wined for him, as he played her pleasure as if it was his favorite musical instrument. Her moans came out as a beautiful melody, which was music to his ears.

Though he wasn't the only one listening! While the excitement had completely taken over they never realized that they never closed the door to the bedroom. Layla had made the mistake of walking into the bedroom, looking for one of her host. She had forgot where they said the towels were so she could take a quick shower before bed. She heard the water running once she stepped into the room, and just as she decided to turn around she heard a sound that was oh so familiar to her. The sound of another woman being pleasured, she wanted to just go back to her room and wait patiently. Unfortunately there was another part of her body that was in control at this point. On top of that her curiosity was peaked, and we know what curiosity does! She stepped closer to the bathroom and as she got closer Asia's moans grew louder. Layla could feel the heat coming from the shower as she came closer to the door. She couldn't stop herself at this point she wanted to see, as a matter of fact she had to see! Peeking around the door she realized that even being in the master bath wasn't close enough for her to see. Taking a couple more steps in she peeked around the wall of the shower room, by this time Asia had complete control of Terrance's head. Keeping a tight grip on the back of his head as she road his lips to ecstasy, her eyes rolled back to their regular position as she turned her head slightly. She wanted to see her husband as he worked, but out of the corner of her eye she noticed that they had company. Asia loosened her grip on her husband, as she looked at Layla giving her an inviting look then a smile. Layla didn't need much more than that to feel invited to the festivities. But Asia wasn't ready to share just yet, she wanted to be sure that it was okay with her partner first. Releasing her husband's head a bit more allowing him to look up at her face she pointed out their guest who by now stood out in the open. Without as much as a sound she mouthed the words "Can she?" to which Terrance happily responded "The more the merrier!" then happily went back to town on her lower region. Asia motioned for their guest to come in and join them, as Layla snatched away her clothes allowing them to fall to the floor she stepped into the shower room immediately hit by the steam as she entered. Walking over to the couple Layla's ample assets slowly getting wetter with each step she took. Finally arriving she immediately cupped one of Asia's breast then leaned in and slid her tongue across her lips. The shock of having two people attacking both sets of her lips at the same time sent waves through Asia's body as she let out a serious moan! She was paralyzed by the pleasure unable to move as her two assailants pleased her body. Terrance moved up from her lower paradise running his moistened bottom lip from her waist to her breast slow and steady. Taking extra time to enjoy her nipples as he teased, played and watched as his wife enjoyed the soft full lips of another woman. Layla caressed Asia's body as she returned the favor to Layla with one hand and grabbing her husband's throbbing member with the other. She couldn't wait to feel his thickness deep inside her wet and wanting pool of juices. Breaking the kiss that was shared between her and Layla to look deep into her husbands eyes. She had one simple request for her husband!

"Fuck Me!!!"

The Congregation

Terrance looked forward to making sure that her request was granted. But before he had the pleasure Layla slid down Asia's body caressing her most intimate places. Reaching her waist and following her waist line from the right side of her body over to the left. Removing her lips and tongue from Asia's body and on to Terrance's thickness. He immediately felt the warmth of her tongue and mouth engulf his meaty member. As she rhythmically moved her head back and forth taking more of him into her mouth each time. Terrance passionately kissed his wife, as each one of the trio became more aroused by the second. Asia was so over taken by the moment that she placed her hand on the back of Layla's head helping her to go back and forth as Layla pleasured her husband. The excitement of it all was beginning to be too much for Terrance as he almost let himself go at that very moment. Gently removing himself from her mouth he slid his hands beneath her arms and helped her up from her squatting position. Leading the women from the shower back into the bedroom still dripping wet from the water wasn't a concern of anyone at the time. The couple insist that Layla lay across the bed and spread her legs. Asia was in the mood to return the southern hospitality Layla had shown her. Climbing up between Layla's outstretched legs and dipping her face down into her wetness. Terrance stood in amazement for just a second enjoying the view before him, but not too long after all he had a request to fulfill.

His wife was in perfect position to feel every stroke he had to offer, and tonight it would definitely be more than what she was use to. Starting off slow as he got deep inside her warmth, allowing himself to enjoy her depths as he watched his wife devour her meal. The expression etched across Layla's face indicated that she was pleased by the work Asia was doing. And the moans released between breaths let Terrance know that he was just as pleasing to Asia. Spreading her ample cheeks in order to better view himself traveling in and out of her beauty Terrance was turned on even more. Asia responded to him, just as a Twinkie would if it was squeezed. Releasing her cream all over his thickness, she couldn't control herself as time went on. Layla wanted to get a closer view of the pleasure that Terrance was administering. Removing herself from beneath Asia, she got on her knees then leaned over Asia. Taking in the magnificent angle wasn't enough she wanted to feel like she was a part of the action. Reaching up to take on some of the responsibilities, she grabbed Asia's cheeks and pulled them apart allowing Terrance to concentrate on giving his wife every inch of himself. It also allowed her to catch a full view of every motion. The pleasure had more than fulfilled Asia's request as she buried her face into the mattress, and clinched the comforter tightly. Asia had done something in that moment that she couldn't remember her husband ever making her do. He was still hard at work while Asia was tapping out, her orgasm was so immense that she collapsed soon after. She needed time to recover from that much pleasure, as she laid face down in a puddle of her own juices legs still quivering from the experience. Terrance stood at the edge of the bed with an accomplished look on his face as he looked down at Layla as her mouth massaged the remnants of Asia off of his thickness. According to the two of them the night had just begun, and in that moment the couple had killed two birds with one stone. They found out that Terrance would indeed be able to keep his wife satisfied, and in doing so answered Layla's ending questions of the night.

After the night that Roslyn enjoyed with Chris she was looking forward to rolling over and starting all over again. Unfortunately when she rolled there was no one there. There was no sign of him or even that he had been there. Well there was a sign of him being there he wrote a note and left it on the bathroom mirror. Letting her know that he would be back to pick her up for their date at 2:00pm. Roslyn smiled then turned to walk back to her bed, her legs still a bit weak from the workout they had the night before. Wondering where exactly he planned to take her this afternoon so she could dress appropriately. She decided a quick text message would certainly do the trick.

"So what should my attire be for this date? Should I be casual or do I need to dress to impress?"

It seemed to take forever for Chris to respond, but after some time passed she received his simple response.

"Don't have to be too dressy, but not too casual either. If that helps."

His response was about as confusing as their rendezvous just hours ago. Roslyn was still not completely sure what it was that had drawn her to him. At the party it seemed like it was the best way to get back at Mark, but what she couldn't understand was how it was he ended up at her place that night? On top of that he didn't even take the time to stay for a morning session. Though she was use to it from the men she had been with in her past. For some reason it had been hard for her to find a man who didn't already have someone in his life. She was constantly drawn to men in some type of relationship. It had been a continuous cycle since her early teen years. She yearned for attention and it didn't matter who she got it from, well at least not from her perspective. After all she wasn't the one in a relationship, they were cheating not her. Being totally honest ninety percent of the time men in relationships fit her lifestyle so much better. Between school, work, and the internship she didn't have time for anything serious. More importantly was that her emotional state didn't have her prepared for any other situation either. So the fact that the men she dealt with were already emotionally attached to someone else, only had small amounts of availability, and they were fun was right up her alley. Most importantly they were someone else's problem! This way suited her just great except for that pesky ten percent of the time when she yearned to be held. Yearned to be made love to, instead of just being fucked. She yearned to be number one, instead of just what she was.

It was already noon, and she knew she had a bit of getting ready to do. So she decided to get herself out of bed and get ready. She intended on getting a certain reaction out of Chris when he came back to pick her up this afternoon.

Isaac woke this morning with intent on getting the answers he had been looking for. He had a strong feeling that the sign that he needed for God to give so badly would be given. And there was only one place he could possibly get that sign from. Picking up the phone and calling his mother, he was surprised by Jason answering.

"Hey! What are you doing home?"

"Needed a break I've been here all week! I've been calling you but haven't been able to get through. You been okay?"

"Yeah of course! Just been pretty busy!"

"No problem! So were you calling for mom? You know she's getting ready for church! I swear it takes three hours for her to get ready. You and I both know Pastor Coleman's sermon only last about thirty minute. So she takes this long and the actual event only last a fraction of that time."

"Yeah but you know it's always been like that. We should be use to it by now."

"Yeah you right we should be but you know how that goes. So do you want me to give her the phone?"

"No that's okay I'll see you guys at church. I was just making sure they were gonna be on time."

"Okay so is Veronica gonna be there too?"

"Umm...........Uh...Yeah I think she is coming but I think we're driving separately today. She has an event today."

"Okay cool! I'll see y'all there!"

Isaac hung up the phone, and fell back unto the bed, wondering if that was the sign he had been waiting for. He knew he had asked for a clear and unequivocal sign, but if this was it why was there still so much guess work involved.

Even knowing that today's service was just the afternoon Mark and his family were some of the first people to arrive. Without having the responsibility of teaching bible school for the young people of the church Mark still had a great deal work to do. Pastor Coleman had an unbelievably dependency on Mark, and it had been that way ever since Mrs. Coleman had passed away some years ago. The sudden death had struck them both unbelievably hard, and though Pastor Coleman never truly showed the pain he felt. Mark could tell that it was there, from that moment on Mark had been constantly at his father's beck and call. He had always been the son of a preacher and following closely in his footsteps. The death seemed to push everything even faster for Mark. That was until the pregnancy, it caused a rift between them that Mark tried so hard to fix by doing everything his father asked of him.

Amber and Mark sat with the baby in one of the front rows preparing to hear the last sermon of the month. It was definitely going to be special. Pastor Coleman usually gave great sermons, but on the first Sunday, and the last Sunday he always seemed to be in a special place with his sermons. It was like he was in a groove, or in the zone and they expected this Sunday to be no different. As they sat there the crowd began to pour in the doors. As Mark and Amber turned their heads to greet the congregation as they entered the sanctuary, seeming to appear from out of no where the organist began to play. Giving the members his rendition of the instrumental to "Total Praise" and if this was any indication to how church was going to be. Then the congregation was in for an unforgettable day, just as the group got comfortable with the organ playing. The choir took their places backing up the exceptional play of the organist. All the stops had been pulled out today. The drummer was there and he had brought a bass playing friend along with him. The choir director was dressed in a fabulous suit with bright accessories, and hair looking better than any female in the building. The petite man stood in front of the choir with the confidence of a true leader. For what he lacked in height he more than made up for in ability, and sass. Raising and lowering hands directing the singers to perfection, this was going to be a great day indeed. As the one of the last groups entered the walls Amber noticed, all her friends. Asia and Terrance brought Layla along for today's word after the night they had just indulged in they could definitely use it too. Veronica was also in the bunch but seemed to be staying to herself, she had on a pair of Mary J sunglasses and an oversized hat. She had her best star that wanted attention, but didn't want to be bothered look going today. She sat way in the back, and was unfortunately too far for Amber to get her attention without causing a scene. She couldn't help but wonder why she wasn't sitting with her husband. After a quick scan of the room Amber figured out why, Isaac was sitting with his mother and brother on the other side of the room about three rows over.

Terrance and the two women that he shared a bed with earlier today sat not too far away from Veronica. Actually about two rows in front of her, their wild night must've had them a bit on the tired side this morning. Asia attempted to wave at both Veronica and Amber with neither of them waving back. Truth was Asia was in such a great mood from the night before that she could care less, well that was until she realized that Veronica and her husband weren't sitting together. She whispered to Terrance to get his attention, when he didn't respond she gave him a slight nudge.

"What's up?"

"I wonder why Veronica and Isaac aren't sitting together?"

"Who knows?"

"Don't you think that's odd?"

"Not really from the looks of it he got here way before her. Maybe she was taking too long getting ready. I know there has been plenty of times I wanted to leave you at home."

"Yeah okay! That's odd, and she was awful quiet yesterday at the house. Remember he never showed up either."

"Okay, okay, calm it down Matlock! She said yesterday he had to work. Don't let your overactive imagination get the best of you. Here's a mystery for you to figure out. Where is that nephew of yours? He promised he would be here today!"

"Well I'm sure he will be here! He probably just got caught up with one of his...........female friends!"

"Yeah well he better get here! I didn't barbeque for nothing yesterday!"

"Oh and here I thought you did that because I asked you to."

"Of course I did babe!"

Pastor Coleman stepped onto the pulpit and took his seat, awaiting his turn to feed the congregation's spirit just as the choir had been doing for the past few moments. The very last group of people were allowed to enter and ushered to their seats before the Pastor stepped to the pulpit. Terrance was happy to see that Chris had made it, and with a surprise guess as well. Roslyn and Chris sat towards the back of the church, but were forced to stand for a second too long. A bunch of the church's women noticed Mr. Alexander and began to whisper. This caused many to take notice, looking to see him and the woman he had brought with him. Even some of the men had to get a glance as well, including Mark and Isaac. Mark broke out in a sweat, and a cough trying to clear his throat and stop himself from choking on his own saliva. Isaac had a totally different reaction for a split second time stood still as he tried to place where he had seen the woman before. At a glance that seemed like so much more, he was unable to place the beautiful woman. Especially not at the distance that he was forced to view her from, and just like that she was gone. She sat down and was blocked of from his view. Cold sweat and all Mark sat preparing for his father to give today's word as the choir brought their song down to a whisper, just as Pastor Coleman approached the microphone.

"Good Mornin' Church!"

"Good morning."

"Today is the Lord's day and we shall rejoice in it!"

"Amen"

"Let us thank the choir for the beautiful melody, and give sister Lyric a special thank you for blessing us with her beautiful voice. Amen!"

"Amen"

"Well today I am not gone take long. But I will be here as long as it takes. Amen!"

"Take ya time!"

"Church I come before you today, with a message in theory. Now I know I don't tend to theorize too much but today, the Lord saw fit to let me. Amen!"

"Mmmm hmmm, preach!"

"Now this one may come as a shock to some of you. But I'm gone say it anyway! We are gone start in the beginning. I know what we get from the text, but bare with me for just a second. Now I may just offend some people today, but I just may have too. Today, I want to take the time to talk about the questions that we have all pondered. The questions that are always sparking up some type of debate. Questions like is GOD black or white? I know, I know the easy way out is he's a spirit and can appear in any form he wishes. Well how about this one is GOD a man or a woman? Well I can tell by the looks on some of the faces that these may be touchy subjects. Amen!"

The church was so quiet that you could hear a pin drop. After which Pastor Coleman paused for several seconds, knowing he was going to continue but a bit unsure as to if he should. With a smirk he started from where he left off.

"Well excuse me gentlemen for not asking you personally could we have a conversation today. But I am sure the ladies are with me so far. Am I right ladies?"

"Preach Reverend!"

"The reason I am so sure is because today I am going to agree with them. Amen! Well listen fella's I'm gonna give it to you straight today. And I plan on standing behind these statements with the word itself. Is that okay? Can I get an Amen!"

Almost under their breath the entire congregation gave Pastor Coleman the Amen that he was so graciously asking for. Even being a little unsure where exactly their pastor was going with today's sermon. They sat patiently and waited for him to continue.

"Well let's start off by looking at some of the Lord's traits. Do ya mind if we list just a few of them? Pull out you pens, we gone learn something today. There are so many examples to support this theory throughout life's instructions manual. But there are a few traits that I want to focus on right now. Is that okay with y'all?"

Pastor Coleman paused for another second as if he was awaiting a response from the members. Scanning the room for a look of disapproval before continuing. Noticing that he had the full support of the women folk, by the ear to ear smiles and nodding of their heads. Though he still had work to do to gain the approval of the men, he was happy to have the women on his side for now.

"Those of you who came prepared pull out your Bible, and those of you who didn't please look on with a neighbor. I want y'all to actually see where I'm going today! And I know some of y'all are gonna want to check behind me after today's sermon. Let's start from the beginning! In Genesis God started off with a plan. She wanted to create something and saw fit to do so, right? In this itself we see the very first act that proves that God is a woman. Now gentlemen let's be honest, just for a second okay! Fellas can I get you to be honest on the Lord's day?"

"Amen! Preach Pastor!"

"Okay we're honest right now! Gentleman, how many of us put plans together? That's not what we do especially not in a singular form! Now if it's a group of us then yes we will sit back and plot and plan, but if it's just one of us by ourselves we don't plan we just do! Am I right? Can I get an Amen?"

The crowd chuckled a bit smiling and laughing briefly as Pastor Coleman continued making his point.

"Now I did say I was gonna prove this theory, and I did say I was gonna tell the truth so let me continue. We find as we continue in Genesis that the Lord took exactly seven days to create the world. Not eight days, not two weeks, God didn't put it off for two weeks. She didn't start today and come back a month later to finish up the work. She worked straight through. Now ladies I have a question for you real quick. And I need you all to be just as honest as we are being today? Ladies how many times have you asked your husband for something simple like take out the garbage and what do we say? We come up with every excuse under the sun don't we? I'll do it in a minute, just give me a second the game is on. Don't let you ask for something a bit more tedious. Don't ask for a bigger project. For example ask him to fix something and a month later you might get him started. Can I get an Amen?"

Once again the church chuckled laughing at the truths that their pastor was taking his time to put out there. A few of the women patrons had to stand up on that point and clap loudly. Pastor Coleman calmed them down, as quickly as he could. Reminding them that they had to go home with that man sitting next to them. With a slight chuckle himself he warned that they better be careful, or they might not get anything done around that house for a long time. With that he continued.

"Now I don't wanna go too far into Genesis because I don't want to confuse you. The only thing I will say is that God saw fit to create Man first then made all the beast of the earth and allowed man to name them all. Then when all was done She saw fit to create Woman from man. Amen!"

The men of the audience finally spoke up in great tone "AMEN!!!" some of them wanted almost looked like they were ready to smack fives like they were at a Pistons game. As if the point that was made was for them.

"See that's exactly why I didn't want to stay in Genesis too long because we would get side tracked and miss the point. Fellas ever wonder were the saying saving the best for last came from?"

Pastor Coleman continued for the next thirty minutes jumping around the Bible picking different aspects and traits of the Lord God. Giving examples of God showing the love that only a mother could express, to God being a jealous God just as women have the ability to be. He also took the time to give an example of God's wrath and vengeance, and how it mirrors that of a woman scorn. Just as he promised he gave a very intriguing outlook on the possibilities of God being a woman. As he reached the climax he finagled his way through connecting all the his points and some way made it all make sense. The basis of the sermon was that women had been blessed with God's traits so intensely that when God created them it was after her own likeness. After his sermon it was extremely hard to find a person that wasn't moved to their feet applauding at today's message. By the end of his work he had even convinced then men of the church that his theory was correct. They especially agreed with the jealousy, and wrath of a woman scorn part.

As the day seemed to be coming to an end Pastor Coleman took the time to acknowledge the visitors. Asking them to stand and if not tell about their own church home, then to at least tell them about the person who had convinced them to visit. He also took time to ask them if they enjoyed the sermon, and opened the doors of the church welcoming them to become members. Chris was sure he had made it past being a visitor, hell he spoke at the Pastor's banquet. He shouldn't have to stand and be put on the spot, but he had been wrong before and this was no different he was wrong again. Terrance gave him a look, and he knew exactly what that meant. Trying to avoid the look of his uncle, Chris acted as if he was so into the words that he couldn't see the stare that was burning a hole through him. Finally as the last person introduced themselves to the congregation, Terrance took matters into his own hands. Standing himself and introducing his nephew and making sure that he would have to stand as well. Chris wouldn't be standing alone as everyone's attention turned to him after he was pointed out by his uncle. Chris quickly gripped the hand of Roslyn and before she could snatch away stood up. Forcing her to stand with him, embarrassed and shy she stood beside the man she barely knew with every eye glued on them. This was just the chance that Isaac was waiting for he would finally get more than just a glimpse of the women. He stared in disbelief! With more wonderment than a child hearing a fairy tale for the first time. It was her! The woman from his dreams, but who was she and why had she been haunting his dreams?

After the quick introduction by Chris of he and his guest thanks to his uncle they returned to their seated positions. Though the damage was done Roslyn had been noticed by Isaac and his interest was peaked. Before bringing an end to today's afternoon service Pastor Coleman opened the floor and the microphone to anyone in the congregation who had a testimony. Usually when this was done there would be a pause, before one of the senior members would rise and walk to the alter to share their testimony. Not today! As the choir started their short version of "I got a testimony!" Veronica raised out of her seat and headed for the alter.

Chapter 18: *Veronica's Vengeance*

"First of I have to thank the church for giving me a home and trying to accept me, through all my struggles and strife. Second I have to thank Pastor Coleman for allowing me the opportunity to be a part of this congregation, and to be one of the lead planners on his birthday event I truly hope everyone knows how thankful I am for the church's support. I'm up here today not to be recognized for my right doing, but to own up to my wrong. Now I wanted to come up and give my testimony, before there was an opportunity to add wood to the fire. As many of you already know...I'm sure. My husband and I are separating. Now don't give me the shocked look now as if some of you didn't already know, and I'm sure if the leak started where I assume it started most of you know why too. For the past week I have tossed and turned, and tossed and turned in my attempts to sleep. As the Lord spoke to me! Yeah I know we forget sometimes, but he I'm sorry pastor...She speaks to Sinners just as She does to Saints. I was one of them, just like some of y'all out here right now are one of them. One of the ones that thought I was foolin' him by coming to church on Sunday. Prayin' and layin' hands on folks stomping and jumping fakin the holy ghost. But it's a thin line between walkin' it and talkin' it, livin' it and givin' it or just pretendin' it alright. Do we really think we can pull the wool over the Lord's eyes? Do we really think by faking it we can get the same reward? Honestly this is about the realest thing I have ever said, I'm sure. And after this a lot of folks won't like me no more, but after this I have to go answer to my Lord!

The Congregation

So with that said let me get y'all out the way! My husband is a wonderful man, a special man and above all else he is a God fearing man. If there is one flaw to this man, it would be that he doesn't have the heart to stand up to the one woman that has her nails dug so deep into him she will never let go. Let me tell you more, about this beautiful man I married and his.........Mother!

I'm sure you all have your respective feeling about Mrs. Patton-Silver, and whether you ever let those feeling be known or not. I have to confess my true feelings for this woman. As my grandmother always told me. She would always say "Baby there are two sides to every stone." Now like most young people I didn't know exactly what she meant when she said that, but I heard what she said. Once I actually met my mother-in-law, I truly had a better understanding. Most rocks have a smooth side, easy to slide your hands across. That's Mrs. Patton-Silver smooth to the touch always there to do the right thing. There with the right connection, smiling for the right people, always at the right function. She is always in the right place at the right time to smooth things over. A little too smooth if you ask me! Because when you flip that rock over you run across that other side. That rough and jagged side of the rock, the side you don't want to brush up against. That's the side that I know! The side that a few of you here have run into, but refuse to speak on because it might hurt the church in some way. You never know when you might need the great Mrs. Patton-Silver! Let's talk for a minute about that rough side, the side that you don't want to cross paths with. The side that refuses to let go of the son's life. The side that still attempts to control everyone around her. Let's talk about the hateful, spiteful side of this woman for a second."

The Congregation sat paralyzed by the words coming from Veronica's mouth. Some not able to believe the way she openly discussed the evilness of her mother-in-law. Others just sat because the gossip that would follow this was too much to pass on. They wanted to hear more as Veronica continued.

"Some of you already know the things I speak of, then to some of you all this is breaking news at eleven. Well how about I tell you something that none of you knew. Hell something I myself didn't know!"

Isaac stood in shock as his wife stood in front of the entire church ready to expose him and his mother for the entire Congregation. Frozen with fear part of Isaac wanted to stop her, while the other part of him wanted nothing more than to let her finish. Isaac wanted her to give him the freedom that he could never obtain himself.

"My husband has a child! And he has had a child for as long as I have known him! I'll do you one better he and his mother have kept this secret for the last fourteen years. But let's be honest was it all of our business maybe, then again maybe not they did it out of fear. Fear of judgment, fear of pressure, fear of failure. Maybe it was because a crazed mother put so much pressure on her son to be perfect that when he finally failed to live up to those expectations she couldn't handle it! She refused to allow that to be the case, she was hell bent on changing the problem."

If no one else would stop her Mrs. Payton-Silver refused to just sit around and listen to her whorish daughter-in-law pull apart the life decisions she had made for her family.

"How dare you stand up there and fix your mouth to judge me! You have no idea what it takes to be me! No idea of the struggles I have had to overcome, the things I have had to endure. You dare get up in front of these people and try to attack me! What right do you have? You..... The biggest mistake my son has ever made. You are a shell of a woman, and don't deserve to kiss the ground that he walks on!"

"You are so right Mother Dearest! I don't deserve that man, and I truly wish I did, I wish he knew how much I would love to be worthy of his love! I'm not sure if you heard or what you've heard, but this is my time to tell the truth. My husband is leaving me, and for good reason as well. I'm pregnant but it's not his child that I am pregnant with. I have been unfaithful to the one man who cherished me, who loved me. The man that put me before all others and took my hand in marriage. Unfortunately this is the same man who couldn't tell me his deepest darkest secret, he couldn't tell me that he couldn't have kids because of an operation that his Mother convinced him to have! The mother that couldn't realize that I was the one person who made him feel special. That I was the one person that brightened his day. The same man who couldn't tell me that the younger brother that I thought he had was actually his son!

So there you have it! My big secret and their even bigger secret! And it's all the truth! Say whatever you will about me, but know that my conscience is clear. Then ask yourself if you can say the same thing?'
'

By the time Veronica finished her confession all eyes were locked on Mrs. Payton-Silver. She sat there in her seat finally feeling the judgment that she tried so hard to avoid all her life. The thing that hurt the most was the blank stare that she received from Isaac. As he stood feet cemented to the ground lost in his own thoughts, not sure if it was actually hearing it for the first time aloud. Or if it was hearing it from someone other than his mother. Was it the different spin his wife had put on the entire situation that had his insides turning. What ever it was

Isaac's devastation was building. As he turned his attention from his mother to Jason who sat in disbelief. Reaching his hand out to the young man who until this day knew Isaac as the best older brother he could ever imagine having.

Sitting and listening to the entire testimony Chris sat with a look of disbelief, but Roslyn had an all together different look etched across her face! She was entranced as if she knew the story all too well. As she stared at Isaac standing there falling apart she couldn't help but feel his pain. Without warning she rose from her seat, without a soul noticing with the exception of Chris.

"Where are you going?"

Not a word in response, Roslyn started walking towards Isaac's side of the church. The closer she came to the front the more eyes followed her. Isaac's daze broke as he looked up at her. She was finally close enough to view her face completely. It couldn't be! As she finally made it close enough for him to see the aged face of Roslyn, well at least it was aged compared to the way he remembered her. Just then Mrs. Patton-Silver rose from her seat immediately forgetting that she was in the Lord's house she did the unthinkable.

"Hell No! What in the hell are you doing here? You promised! We had an agreement! What the hell are you doing!"

All Isaac could mutter was "Oh my GOD!"

Roslyn, walked past their area to the very front of the church excusing Veronica from the microphone. Eyes filled with tears she hugged Veronica, before taking the microphone from her to address the crowd. Explaining that she wasn't here to cause problems, but she could understand how Veronica felt. She could understand the pain that Mrs. Patton-Silver was able to cause. She knew first hand how it felt to have her constantly riding her, how much pressure she could put on someone. How it felt to not have the support you needed, when the mother of the man you loved constantly attacked you verbally. Telling you at every turn that you weren't worthy, and how her son was too good for you. She knew just how devious Mrs. Patton-Silver could be, and wondered if her son knew himself. Turning her attention to him looking directly at him, as he stood looking shameful.

"You never wondered about me? Never came looking for me, but you said you cared! You never came to my defense when she attacked me! You never corrected her when she said I wasn't good enough! I see some things don't change with age!

You allowed her to believe that I was just a leach, a dirty slut who wasn't good enough. You let her tell me that I was just trying to latch onto you because you were going places. You allowed her to say it so much that I started to believe it! So much that I became it, and when she came to my room with the offer I took it!"

By this time the tears were streaming down her face, the words were jammed together. As she tried to keep herself together, but it wasn't working she was falling apart with each word she spoke. The armor that she had built, over the years was unable to maintain its strength in her time of need. As she started to lower the microphone she felt a comforting touch. With a tight embrace, Veronica gave her the strength that she needed the support that she so badly needed. It was enough for her to finish what she came up there to do.

"She came to the room not five minutes after I had delivered. I hadn't even held my son yet, hadn't even touched him, not even seen him. And she was already there with her devilish offer! Telling me how you didn't want to be bothered with me. Telling me how you felt like I was trying to trap you, and ruin your future. Telling me how I didn't really want to be a single mother, and how I was too young for the responsibility. Reminding me of how hard it would be, how cold the world would be. Reminding me of how I would end up just like my mother! How I would resent the baby for ruining my life, for stealing my youth. But she said she could save me! She could give the baby a better life, and give me my life back. All I had to do was take this check and disappear! All I had to do was promise to never come back, never bother her perfect family again. So I did it! I took the money, because that's all you ever expected of me anyway. I was just a leach!

Dropping the microphone to the floor Roslyn walked away, without another peep. She didn't take the time to even look their way again. She walked out of the church feeling as though a weight was lifted off her shoulders. The guilt that she was caring was finally taken away, the secret that she had been holding on to for the past fifteen years was no more. She was finally free!

As she walked out the door Isaac finally found his voice, screaming her name, or at least the one he knew her by...."Sherita!!!"

Standing there in a state of disbelief, Isaac devastated from the words he had just heard. He knew his mother was a master of manipulation but would she really go this far...Would she be this devious...Even more disturbing was the fact that Jason was hearing all this for the very first time. As Isaac turned and looked into his son's eyes he was faced with a lifetime of disappointment. Reaching out his hand Isaac attempted to grab his son to no avail. Jason removed himself from his seat and ran for the doors of the church. Left with nothing more than the face that started it all staring at him without a hint of remorse, Isaac dropped his hand then his head and walked away. Leaving Mrs. Patton-Silver to the mercy of ***The Congregation***.

Book Club Questions

- Who is your favorite character?

- Did you hate any of the characters? Who/Why?

- Did the actions of Mrs. Patton-Silver seem justified?

- If you were Amber would you have stayed with Mark?

- Do you agree with the decision made by Terrance and Asia to seek help? Do you think you would've made a similar decision?

- Where you surprised by the secrets that Veronica and Isaac kept from each other?

- Did the plot suck you in or did you have to force yourself to read the book?

- Do the characters seem real and believable? Can you relate to their predicaments? To what existent do they remind you of yourself or someone you know?

- How do the characters change or evolve throughout the course of the story? What events trigger such changes?

- How does this book compare to other books written by this author?

Author's Titles

KARMA

(Kar-ma - The sum of a person's actions during the successive phases of his or her existence, regarded as determining his or her destiny in future incarnations.) ***Karma*** is all around us, affecting our everyday lives, we're absorbed by it. It's as real as the air we breathe, and the love we share. Just like the love we feel and the air we breathe it's going on without being seen. No one is more affected by this than Christopher. After years of sexual escapades, breaking hearts, and in the end ruining good women over and over again, he thought that he had finally found "the one". There was something different about her, she was special. So special in fact that instead of her being head over heels for him like so many others before her, it was the complete opposite. It was she that had him wide open, and in the end it would be him that would have to pick up the pieces of his broken heart, and find a way to go on.

THE LEARNING CURVE

Christopher Alexander is back and out for revenge. After being hurt in an unimaginable way he's out to make them pay. The only problem is he plans on making all of women pay for the decision of one woman.

Author, Hashim Conner starts The Learning Curve exactly where Karma left off. Instead of attempting to put the pieces back together and heal, Christopher dives head first back into a life of sexual encounters turning his sex life into some kind of game with rules that only he's privy to. Christopher runs from woman to woman, until he's broadsided by Ariel who's playing a game herself.

With her indecisiveness she has an impossible task of choosing between Christopher and her ex who isn't ready to let her go. Without much effort at all she has Christopher back in a position that he swore he would never be in again. From the classroom, to the bedroom, Christopher gives us a much deeper look into the exciting life he lives.

Author's Bio

Hashim Conner was born and raised in Detroit Michigan, by the three women who kept him in line. His Grandmother Rosie Cook, Grandmother Lydia Alexander, and biggest fan, his mother Shirley Stephenson without whom none of his success would be possible. These women help shape the man before you, by pushing him to greater heights than he knew were possible. Hashim graduated Samuel L. Mumford High School, and then went on to earn his Associates in Communications from Wayne County Community college and his Bachelor's Degree from Wayne State University. All the while taking time out to enjoy the art of writing, which he fell in love with at the tender age of nine. Hashim has accomplished the task of not only publishing KARMA, his first book, which is the prequel to The Learning Curve, but he also has plans for a third part to this trilogy which will be titled THE ESCORT.

Author Information:

Website: www.hashimconner.net

http://conversations-with-hashimconner.blogspot.com

Email: hcconner@yahoo.com